KU-376-172

About the Author

Eileen Dunlop was born and went to school in Alloa, Clackmannanshire, Scotland, near where she now lives. She has published a number of novels for children, of which *The House on the Hill* (1987) was commended for the Carnegie Medal, *Finn's Island* (1991) commended for the McVitie's Prize for the Scottish Writer of the Year and *The Maze Stone* (1982) and *Clementina* (1985) won Scottish Arts Council Books Awards.

She has also, with her husband Antony Kamm, written several information books on Scottish themes, and compiled two collections of verse. She is the author of *Tales of St Patrick*, *Tales of St Columba*, *Stones of Destiny*, *Waters of Life*, *The Ghost by the Sea*, *Warrior's Bride*, *Ghoul's Den*, *The Haunting of Alice Fairlie* and *Nicholas Moonlight* all published by Poolbeg, and has contributed short stories to three horror anthologies: *Shiver*, *Chiller* and *Nightmares*, also published by Poolbeg. *Ghoul's Den* was shortlisted for the RAI awards in 2001.

Also by Eileen Dunlop

Nicholas Moonlight
The Haunting of Alice Fairlie
The Ghost by the Sea
Ghoul's Den
Warrior's Bride
Tales of St Columba

To May, Jennifer and John

Contents

1.   The Road to Weerdwood   1
2.   The Worst Fright   8
3.   Piggy Gillanders   13
4.   In the Garden   21
5.   A Family Face   28
6.   Sharing a Secret   36
7.   Jake's Story   41
8.   Three of Us   49
9.   Breakthrough   56
10.   What Grace Saw   64
11.   At Sutor Point   73
12.   The Woman in White   79
13.   Absent Without Leave   87
14.   Old Clothes   96
15.   A Chill in the Night   103
16.   The Co-Walker   109
17.   Looking for Harriet   117
18.   The Treasure Hunt   123
19.   In Two Minds   129
20.   Possessed   137
21.   Grey   144
22.   The Power of Names   151
23.   Temporary Friends   164

1

The Road to Weerdwood

I can remember exactly the moment when my confidence cracked and I wished, far too late, that I hadn't been so pig-headed. Until then I'd been really upbeat; I'd enjoyed the weekend and arrived at school on Monday morning feeling relaxed and positive. I'd grabbed a window seat in the minibus and waved a cheerful goodbye to Mum. On the drive through Fife I'd admired the greening woods and red-roofed farms, and I'd had the warm, expectant feeling you have when a cherished dream is about to come true. It was as we left the carpark in Perth after a toilet stop that my mood changed, like a switch flicking suddenly from light to dark. As Miss Gallacher swung the minibus out onto the road, I felt a breathless panic that reminded me of the asthma attacks I was supposed to have outgrown.

Don't be so stupid, I told myself furiously. *You've been looking forward to this for months, haven't you? What's changed, except the weather?*

The weather had certainly changed, as abruptly and unpleasantly as my frame of mind. While we'd been in the loo, the shy spring sun had been zapped by a scud of dark grey cloud. As the minibus joined the traffic streaming north, the last tatters of blue sky vanished. Random flicks of water on the windows quickly multiplied and soon rain was rattling like dried peas on the roof. As the city thinned out into a patchwork of fields, I peered nervously through the bleary glass. My alarm intensified as I saw the fields being squeezed between tall, spruce-clad mountains. They looked like ugly giants with snow streaking their crowns and mist wafting round their shoulders like damp grey hair.

"Isn't this the pits? We must be crazy," I moaned to Gillian, who was slumped on the seat beside me.

Probably it was just as well that she had her Walkman switched on and couldn't hear me. I reckon the word "We" would have had her spluttering indignantly. Gillian was one of several people who thought the only person cracked was me.

"You, Con Carberry? Well, I *am* surprised."

That was Mrs Mackay, our sarky PE teacher, who'd been trying for two years to prise me out of my coat and onto the hockey pitch.

"You do know we'll be away almost three weeks, don't you, Con?" That was Miss Gallacher, our form tutor, who was to be in charge of the group from Underwood Academy. Her lips twitched as she added, "Have you forgotten how homesick you were the day we went to Edinburgh Zoo?"

My best friend, Gillian Croft, had been even ruder.

"You've no muscles, you wear two vests in August and you don't like getting your hands dirty," she'd said.

So yes, I had been warned. Yet as I plucked a magazine from my tote bag and turned my shoulder to the window of the minibus, I was completely bewildered. I'd been so sure of myself and I'd looked forward to the trip so much. Why, when I was at last on my way, should I be gripped so cruelly by tentacles of foreboding and fear?

Hindsight is a wonderful thing. Later on, I would see my perverse attraction to Weerdwood and my panic attack on the bus as early incidents in a stupendously spooky affair, but how could I know that at the time? The one certain thing was that, the minute I'd looked in the information pack and seen the arty sepia photograph of an old mansion house in a bare winter garden, I'd wanted to go there more than I'd ever wanted anything in my life.

Come and share the Weerdwood Experience! Help other people and have a load of fun! The Weerdwood Trust offers work experience to young teenagers in a secure and friendly environment, supervised by qualified staff, at Weerdwood House on the Cromarty Firth . . .

Mum, on the day when I rushed home waving the information pack, was clearly baffled.

"I don't think you'd like it, Con," she frowned. "It's very cold up north in March and you're not exactly an outdoor type. You won't even walk the dog when it's raining.

Besides –" her dark eyes scanned me anxiously "– I really can't imagine you painting walls and working in a garden. I know your asthma's better, but no one would call you sturdy."

I made a big effort to conceal my impatience.

"It says in the pack that we'll be assessed when we arrive," I pointed out. "Nobody will be asked to do work they're not fit for." Then, to head off some other objection, I added longingly, "I just think the whole thing sounds so cool."

I meant it, too. Time out of school wasn't to be sneezed at and I did think it would be cool, living with other kids in part of an old house and helping to turn the rest into a holiday centre for disabled people. OK, it would be hard work, but there would be treats, like evening sessions of music, indoor games and a treasure hunt. There would be a Saturday trip to Inverness for shopping and ten-pin bowling, and swimming at a leisure complex nearby.

"I have to take the consent form back tomorrow," I went on urgently. "Miss Gallacher says Underwood Academy has only been offered twelve places, so it'll be 'First come, first served'. Oh, *please*! We only have to pay for the minibus and I'm dying to go." Then, with Mum still looking leery, I played my trump card. "Remember you and Mark were talking about a winter holiday," I said slyly, "but you didn't want to take me out of school? Well, now's your chance, eh?"

A gratifying gleam came into Mum's eye. Mark's my stepfather and, because he's a nice guy and my real father's dead, he walks on eggs trying to include me in everything. He and Mum even took me on their honeymoon, for God's sake.

"I'll talk to Mark. We'll think about it," Mum said.

Next morning Mum dropped me off at the school gate on her way to the travel agent. Where should they go? Crete or Sardinia? Oporto or Alicante? Just then I couldn't have cared less. The minute Assembly was over, I rushed up to Miss Gallacher's room with my consent form – unnecessarily, as it turned out. From our class of thirty, only nine were keen to give the Weerdwood Experience a whirl. The rest were either too hip or too attached to their own tellies and duvets to respond to the challenge of painting and bagging garden rubbish on a windswept headland above a wintry Highland firth.

"Maybe it's the name, Weerdwood, that puts them off," suggested Gillian as we walked home in the moist November afternoon. "It's sort of – well, weird, you know."

It had been no surprise when Gillian brought back her consent form. She was confident, athletic and not very imaginative, the kind of person who always gets "Shows leadership potential" written on her report. I was surprised that someone so sensible would say anything so silly.

"They have no spirit of adventure," I said loftily.

"Unlike you, Con," said Gillian, trying not to laugh.

The magazine I'd brought to read on the minibus didn't hold my attention. I was sick of articles about Ali G and Prince William, while the offers of free lip-glosses and fake tattoos left me cold. Beyond bleak Drumochter I ate a chocolate bar and watched forest give way to moorland so black that it looked like the aftermath of a great burning. Passing cars had their headlamps on and windscreen wipers were working overtime against the sleet. Since everyone around me seemed to be zonked, I closed my eyes, but I was too edgy to sleep. Too late, uneasy questions scratched my mind. Why, in the long weeks between November and March, had I never once wished I was going to Portugal with Mum and Mark? Why had it never occurred to me that the name 'Weerdwood' was weird? Why hadn't I been spooked by my repetitive, misleading dreams?

In the dreams, it was always summer at Weerdwood. The garden was bright with poppies, lupins and Canterbury bells and the old house glowed with fresh, honey-coloured paint. As I stood on the lawn, I heard music and laughter tumbling from windows open to the warm evening air. Sometimes I dreamt I was inside the house, climbing a stone stair and wandering through tall rooms with peacock wallpaper and ornate, gilded chairs. Above a white marble fireplace, a golden-haired young woman in a white dress, her hand laid gently on the head of a large grey dog, gazed out from a heavy gold frame. These dreams weren't scary, but wasn't it strange to have had them almost every night?

Only once I'd dreamt something that frightened me. Standing on the paved forecourt, I'd looked up at a window above the front door and glimpsed a face I'd recognised. But with a swish of a velvet curtain it had vanished, and by morning I'd forgotten it. Only on the minibus, barely thirty miles from Weerdwood, did that brief flash of nightmare return to me, triggering a string of images so disturbing that I writhed on the seat, trying desperately to swallow the terror bubbling in my throat.

"Are you all right, Con?" Gillian's concerned voice seemed to come from far away. "You're not going to be sick, are you?"

I shook my head, but my lips were too unstable to frame a reply. Leaning back, I gulped the stale, overused air.

Breathe deeply, I ordered myself. *It was only a dream. You haven't seen him for years and you'll never have to see him again.*

I pulled myself together, but, as the minibus sped across a long bridge suspended over the steely water of the Moray Firth, I was uncomfortably aware that I'd passed a point of no return. Right now, Mum and Mark were on their way to Glasgow Airport. In four hours they'd be in Lisbon and I'd need a better reason than spooky feelings for summoning them back. Whatever lay ahead, I must try to cope with it alone.

2

The Worst Fright

Perhaps because oppressive moors and mountains had given way to a more gentle landscape, beyond Inverness I had a brief respite from terror. As evening approached the sky cleared quite suddenly and, as the minibus purred along a smooth coastal road, weak sunshine glinted on shingle laid bare by the ebb tide. There was an oil-rig out in the river mouth and gulls swooping over water grey and crinkly as an elephant's skin. It was so calm and unthreatening that momentarily I felt ashamed of myself. Only when Miss Gallacher called, "Look, everyone! That's Weerdwood!" and I saw the tall, honey-coloured house dodging behind a screen of silver birch, did apprehension again grip my mind.

My classmates seemed enviably relaxed. As Miss Gallacher manoeuvred the minibus through iron gateposts, they unbuckled their seat belts. While unpruned branches scraped the windows along a pot-holed drive, they yawned and stretched, zipping up their jackets and cramming tapes and soft drinks cans into their bags. Opinions were voiced: "Jeeze, what a tip! Whose bright idea was this, by the way?"

"Look! It's got a belfry. I bet it's got bats in it."

"Miss, can you just turn round and go home again?"

"I hope the tea's ready. I'm starving."

The only words that impinged on me were Gillian's.

"Fancy – the house actually is yellow. I thought that was just a photographer's trick and it would really be grey."

"No. I knew it was yellow," I heard myself reply, though I really had no more reason to know this than she had.

I let everyone else get out before me, but eventually I too had to climb out into the chilly March dusk. While the others shuffled glumly and Miss Gallacher sorted out the luggage, I squinted, half reluctant and half curious, at the old house. The contrast between the Weerdwood of my dreams and the one I saw was painful. In reality the painted pebbledash was damp and scabrous with neglect, the elegant sash windows dusty and disfigured by broken panes. The crumbling steps leading up to the battered front door were choked with weeds, and tears of disappointment welled in my eyes. I didn't want to go on looking, yet when Miss Gallacher said, "This way, everyone," and strode confidently up the steps in her checked trousers and size-eight boots, once again I was last to move.

This was because I had noticed something disturbing. In the row of five first-floor windows, there was a blank. The window above the door, where in a nightmare I'd seen someone I knew, had been roughly bricked up and painted black. It was hideous and shocking, like a crudely patched eye on a dignified face. Just wondering what lay behind it made me weak at the knees.

Only when I heard Gillian calling from the doorway, "Come on, Con, or you'll be locked out," did I heave up my rucksack, grab my tote bag and hurtle after her into the faintly lit hall.

It's sad to think that, if I hadn't been spooked out of my mind, I'd really have enjoyed the surprise waiting for us. Weerdwood's derelict façade gave no clue as to what we'd find inside; in fact the whole west wing, which lay at right angles to the main house, had already been restored as a residential centre. When Miss Gallacher, who knew the place well, had led us down a dark corridor and opened a door with 'Admiral's Lodge' painted on it, warmth and light sprang out to meet us. We heard a radio playing Classic FM, and saw youngish people in casual clothes popping through other doors around a square entrance hall.

"Here they are now!"

"You didn't crash the minibus then, Julie?"

"Welcome to Weerdwood, kids. Dump your bags and come into the sitting-room. Rusty will get you sorted out."

From the sitting-room, where there was a log fire and a circle of comfortable chairs, we could glimpse a shiny kitchen. A young woman in a white overall was busy preparing supper.

At one end of the sitting-room, an open door revealed a dining-room with blue walls and checked gingham tablecloths. The place was really cool and I could see relief on other faces. Only my pleasure was dimmed by fear.

A brown-bearded young man in jeans and a grey shirt – "My name's Rusty but you can call me Boss" – came with a clipboard and read out the numbers of our bedrooms. "Lucy Paul and Gemma Barker, you're in Room 2. Gillian Croft, Con Carberry and Anne Paley, you're in Room 3. Boys, you're all in the attic. Grab your gear and follow me."

While the four boys sloped off with Rusty, the girls followed Miss Gallacher up a narrow, carpeted stair.

"I'm in Room 1 if you need me," she said.

Actually, even I thought our room was lovely, with red and white striped duvets, matt aluminium reading lamps and neat pine wardrobes. From the window we could see the glow of a town staining the night sky, and the fractured reflection of the oil-rig's lights on the dark water.

"I like this," said Gillian approvingly, heaving her rucksack on to one of the beds. "Let's get unpacked, then we'll find out when the other school's arriving. If they're sharing our shower, we'll have to make up a rota."

Anne Paley made a face at Gillian's back, but I ignored her. She wasn't really a friend of mine and, to tell the truth, I found Gillian's cheerful bossiness reassuring. Thin and frankly mouse-like, I reckoned I'd have been bullied at school without the protection of tall, breezy Gillian. As I hung up my trousers and pushed sweaters and underwear into a drawer, I was thankful she was there. But as I

11

showered and put on fresh clothes, I kept seeing the ugly, bricked-up window in my mind.

A strong smell of cheesy pasta was floating through the house. At any other time it would have made my mouth water, but now, although I hadn't eaten much since breakfast, I didn't want any supper. But rather than rile Miss Gallacher, who already thought I was wet, I went downstairs with the other girls. A dark young woman, who would have looked good in something less nerdy than a faded sweatshirt and limp brown cords, was waiting for us in the hall.

"I'm Jess. You must be starving," she said, with a smile. "Supper's ready in the dining-room. Help yourselves to bread and salad, and Jake will give you some pasta."

If anyone had told me that, after all I'd gone through, the worst fright of the day was still to come, I think I'd have collapsed screaming on the spot. I'd taken a spoonful of coleslaw and a small piece of bread. As I edged up the queue towards the hotplate, I saw a young guy in a white apron slapping pasta onto plates with a long serving spoon. He had closely cropped blond hair and metal ear-studs, and at the sight of his pale, thin-lipped face my mouth went dry and my chest tightened painfully. As I stared he looked up, and I was eyeball to eyeball with the person I'd last seen in a nightmare. He was as shocked as I was. His head jerked and his blue eyes goggled in disbelief.

"Oh, please, God! Not you," he groaned.

3

Piggy Gillanders

Jess had called him Jake, but that wasn't his real name. He was Joseph Drummond Gillanders, and he had lived next door to us in Paisley when I was a little girl. His mother called him Drummond, but to every kid in the street he was known as 'Piggy', which suited him a whole lot better. It wasn't that he looked particularly like a pig. He was actually more like a ferret, pinched in the face and broad at the rump, with pink-rimmed eyes and tufty, almost colourless hair. But he was piggy by nature, if that isn't too big an insult to pigs.

Piggy Gillanders, who was about ten when I was six, had a nature to match his face. He pulled the wings off flies, smashed birds' eggs and crushed frogs under a stone. He had no respect for people either, unless they were a lot bigger and stronger than he was. All the younger kids in Barony Crescent went in fear of his sly kicks and punches, but the worst of his malevolence was, for no understandable reason, reserved for me. I couldn't walk home from school without him jumping out from behind a wall, grabbing my scarf and twisting it until I thought I was going to black out. He tripped me and lit matches and threatened to set fire to my hair. I was so scared of him that the sight of his white face peering through the hedge between our gardens made me physically sick.

Mum knew I had problems. She could hardly help it, with me constantly whingeing and begging her to complain to the head teacher. But, because Piggy was too cunning to attack me in view of my house and because he was careful never to mark me, I honestly think she thought I was exaggerating.

"Let's not make a fuss at the school, pet. I'll speak to Betty," she said, meaning Mrs Gillanders.

Which she probably did, in her downbeat, apologetic fashion, but what difference could it make? Mrs Gillanders doted on Piggy. "He's all I've got," she'd whimper, and Mum felt sorry for her, because she lived on benefit (Piggy's dad having 'taken a job in Southport', or, I thought more likely, scarpered to get shot of Piggy) and she had to take tablets for her nerves.

"Just try to keep out of Drummond's way," suggested Mum feebly. "He'll be going to the High School next year and you won't see him so often."

I stopped complaining then, because by that time Mum had problems of her own. My dad was diagnosed with acute kidney failure when I was seven and a half and for the next eighteen months, while he was on dialysis and waiting for a kidney transplant, Mum's life was stressful enough without me adding to her problems. Eventually the hospital found a donor for Dad, but something went wrong and his body rejected the kidney. I reckon he gave up hope after that, because I only ever saw him lying on the couch in his dressing-gown, sighing and staring into space. By then I hardly recognised the puffy-faced, querulous man my father had become and, when he died three months after his failed operation, I felt little grief. Piggy and his mother came to the funeral. Outside the crematorium they shook hands with Mum and me. Piggy squeezed my fingers so hard that I nearly yelped with pain.

Strangely, I have no memory of seeing Piggy in Barony Crescent after that day, although I must have done, since it was three months before Mum and I moved. We'd only lived in Paisley because of Dad's work, and Mum decided we should have a new start in Gilmerton, the suburb of Edinburgh where she'd been brought up. We'd been there about a year when she met Mark, who was the librarian at the college where she had a part-time secretarial job. They were married the following spring. Mum and Mrs Gillanders exchanged cards at Christmas, which was how we learned that Piggy had come to grief. At the age of fourteen he'd been leader of a gang that torched a primary school. When last heard of, he'd been banged up in a young offenders' unit.

"Poor Betty Gillanders," sighed Mum, in her soft-hearted fashion. "Drummond was all she had."

"He was a rotten pig. He had it coming," I replied stonily.

Stunned by misfortune and disbelief, I sat at a small table with Gillian, Gemma and Lucy. Anne, as usual, was sharing a table with the boys. I couldn't take my eyes off the kitchen door through which Piggy Gillanders had disappeared. As my companions gobbled and giggled, I pushed pasta shells around my plate with a fork and tried feverishly to persuade myself that I'd made a mistake. Perhaps it hadn't really been Piggy serving the supper, but a Piggy-look-alike. Except that a look-alike wouldn't so obviously have known me too. A waking dream, then, I thought hopefully, or a ghost. Perhaps I was mentally ill and hallucinating. Even that bleak analysis seemed preferable to the prospect of almost three weeks trapped in a sinister house at the back of beyond with Joseph Drummond Gillanders.

While we were helping ourselves to fruit and yoghurt from the serving counter, the other group of volunteers arrived. Miss Gallacher had told us on the minibus that they were from Queen Maud's College, an all-girls private school in the north of England – news that had gone down better with the boys than with the girls in our party. They came swinging into the dining-room, six large, confident young women accompanied by a teacher. She was the kind you imagine teaching PE in an old-fashioned school story, red-cheeked and hearty in a Barbour jacket and baggy tweed trousers.

"This way, girls! Take a tray and get in line," she trumpeted, as if they were five-year-olds on their first day at school.

The kitchen door swung open as Piggy slouched out to

fill their plates. Not a hallucination, then. I saw his pale blue eyes flickering round as he tried to locate me, but, encountering my hostile stare, he hastily glanced away. As soon as he'd served the newcomers he slunk back into the kitchen, while they and their teacher formed an exclusive huddle on the other side of the dining-room. Between mouthfuls of pear and banana, Gemma and Lucy criticised their haircuts and their purple uniform tracksuits. Gillian remonstrated in her head-girl-in-waiting tone.

"Don't be so catty, you guys. I'm sure they'll be quite nice when we get to know them."

I nibbled a few grapes and yearned for my bed at home.

Actually, just then any bed would have done. It was after eight before the meal was over, and obviously I wasn't the only one yearning for a hot shower and an early night. When Rusty stood up, banged the table with a spoon and said, "If you'd all like to take a chair in the sitting-room, there are a few things I'd like to go over," enthusiasm didn't exactly fill the air. Sensing the glum atmosphere, he added, "This won't take long. Bed time's normally ten, but we'll let you turn in early tonight."

Stifling yawns, we scraped back our chairs and shambled next door. When we'd each bagged a chair, Rusty, Jess and the young woman I'd seen cooking plonked themselves down beside us. There was one chair left vacant and a moment later Piggy Gillanders, minus his apron, slid himself onto it. He didn't look at me, but I felt my stomach contract, just as it used to when I saw him lurching round the corner of Barony Crescent. Between fear and exhaustion, I don't know how I prevented myself from howling out loud.

"Right," said Rusty briskly, shuffling papers on his knee. "First, some introductions. My name's Robert Cooper, known as Rusty, and I'm employed by the Weerdwood Trust as Warden here. Jess Brooks is my assistant. Mary Royle here cooks for us and this guy is Jake Gillanders. He helps Mary in the kitchen and does odd jobs about the place. Jess and I will be in charge of your work groups, with help from your teachers, Miss Gallacher and Mrs Finch. We'll sort the groups out in the morning, after we've inspected your biceps. It's mostly outdoor work at this time of year, but we've plenty of indoor jobs to keep you busy if the weather turns nasty. Any questions? No? I'll give you our basic rules, then."

He had a sing-song Glasgow accent and, as he intoned a long list of dos and don'ts, I thought – not for the last time – that the Warden of Weerdwood could bore for Scotland. It was all standard stuff: do be punctual for meals, do use the lavatory brush, do switch off the upstairs lights. Don't go into roped-off parts of the house, don't smoke, never go into the opposite sex's sleeping quarters, don't go down on the sands without an adult. Anyone found with alcohol or drugs would be sent home immediately. *Don't tempt me.* My companions' eyes quickly glazed over, but I couldn't take mine off Piggy Gillanders. Although he'd blinked a lot when Rusty mentioned his name, he hadn't moved since he sat down and he certainly wasn't looking at me. His eyes were fixed blankly on a point above the fireplace, and if he was aware of my staring he gave no sign.

I suppose everybody changes between thirteen and

seventeen, but Piggy hadn't changed in the way I'd have expected. He had been a strangely shaped child, peaky-faced and narrow at the shoulders but bulky from the chest down, probably because he ate so many chips and sugary snacks. Perhaps being banged up had made the difference; without his white apron to bulk him out he was as thin as string, his stomach flat and his tight white T-shirt showing clearly the countours of his ribs. Even his face, with its pale eyebrows and pointed nose, seemed more gaunt. His cheekbones stood out starkly and there were dark shadows under his eyes. He didn't look well – as I was observing coldly when a sudden sharpening of Rusty's tone called my attention back to him.

"There's just one more thing, then you can turn in. I'm only mentioning this because you've probably never lived in a big, old house before, and we've had some stupid idiots here recently who thought it was a laugh to upset other people." His face had reddened and his thick eyebrows were twitching with annoyance. "I want you to get this right now," he barked. "This place isn't called Weerdwood because it's weird. It was built in the 1760s by a man called Admiral Lord Weare, who called it Wearewood – W-E-A-R-E-W-O-O-D. The name changed because long ago people couldn't spell, and they wrote things down as they thought they sounded. We have no green ladies, no one with his head tucked underneath his arm and no Hound of the Baskervilles. If you hear a dog barking at night, it's at the farm up the road. Anyone who tells you different is having you on, OK?"

He guffawed fiercely, showing crooked white teeth. Jess and Mary tittered supportively, inviting us to join in. Of course, no one did. My companions sat staring at the Warden of Weerdwood in a mixture of contempt and disbelief. They might as well have had balloons coming out of their heads saying: *"This guy needs a holiday."* Only Piggy, I noticed, wasn't toeing the Rusty line. He was blinking and licking his lips and when, just for an instant, his eyes looked into mine, I saw an expression I recognised as fear.

It was one of the posh girls who broke the silence.

"Well, thank you for that reassurance, Mr Cooper," she said coolly. "Are we allowed to go to bed now?"

There was no doubt that Rusty had made an error of judgment. As we trailed upstairs, all the girls were united in indignation.

"Honestly! What a silly prat!"

"Nobody believes in ghosts nowadays."

"Maybe he should get out more."

"Goodnight, girls. No going *Woo-woo-woo* in the night, remember!"

Of course, I agreed that if anyone was putting stupid ideas into people's heads, it was Rusty. Who, after all, knew better than I did that fear of the visible is far more compelling than anything dreamt up by imagination? So when, after Miss Gallacher had said goodnight and put out the light, I heard dog noises, I wasn't concerned – even though the animal wasn't barking in the distance, but snuffling and scratching in the corridor outside our room. A mournful whine was the last sound I heard before my exhausted body deleted my mind and I dropped down into a long, dreamless sleep.

4

In the Garden

By breakfast time, the brief solidarity of the first night had evaporated. The uniformed girls of Queen Maud's College, who shared rooms along the corridor from ours, had annoyed Gillian by hogging two of the three showers and not even saying "Good morning". In the dining-room they sat apart with their teacher, slurping orange juice and chomping cereal. No one is at their best at a quarter to eight on a wintry morning, and I dare say we looked as hacked off as they did. But I doubt anyone else had a knot of despair in their stomach like the one that was tormenting me.

I hadn't had a bad night, but I'd been lying awake since before six in the grey, maritime morning. Miss Gallacher had opened the curtains when we got into bed, and I could see mist among branches as the light strengthened from the sea. At home I'd imagined my first waking at Weerdwood and the pleasure of knowing that, at last, I was in the house of my dreams. Now I could have wept with self-pity and disillusionment.

Of course, my first thought had been of Piggy, and horror washed over me as I contemplated the long, scary days ahead. I wondered seriously whether I should run away, but, even if I'd had somewhere to go, Miss Gallacher had my pocket money and I'd had it drummed into me how dangerous it was to hitch lifts with strangers. I tried to be calm and consider other options, only to conclude that right now there really weren't any. Mum and Mark wouldn't be home for ten days and, although I had their mobile number, I didn't have a reason they'd respect for asking them to return. I wasn't at death's door and they were in Portugal, for God's sake. Of course I had an emergency contact – or rather Miss Gallacher had; we hadn't been allowed to bring mobile phones to Weerdwood and had been asked not to make 'unnecessary calls'. Part of the 'Weerdwood Experience', apparently, was learning to stand on our own feet. Besides, my emergency contact (because I had no other relative) was my Auntie Morag, who had always thought I was a wimp. I could just imagine her harsh voice crackling indignantly: "Ach, get away, you silly wee lassie! It's time to start crying when you're hurt . . . "

A fat lot she knew about it, or ever would.

My sad thoughts were interrupted by a shrill bell in the corridor. Gillian and Anne stretched and groaned. A minute later Miss Gallacher's curly red head popped round the edge of the door.

"Morning, possums! Rise and shine!"

God, don't you just love teachers? Still, she was there, all twelve stone of her, and so were lots of other people. As I showered and put on grey trousers and a warm blue jersey, I tried to comfort myself with the thought that there was safety in numbers. Surely if I stayed close to Gillian, and fixed things so that I was always within calling distance of an adult, I would be safe enough. Even so, as I went down to the dining-room, the prospect of seeing Piggy dishing up the sausages made my heart knock against my ribs.

Which made it all a bit of an anti-climax that Piggy was nowhere to be seen. It was the cook, Mary, who was behind the serving counter, pouring fruit juice and inviting us to have a bacon roll, or a mushroom and potato cake if we were vegetarian.

"You need a good breakfast if you're going to be working out of doors," she told us. "It helps to keep out the cold."

As I accepted a bacon roll I stood on tiptoe, trying in vain to get a glimpse of my enemy through the round window on the kitchen door. I didn't want to draw attention to myself by asking straight out, "Where's Jake?" so I carried my tray to the table where Gillian was still banging on about how we needed a rota to stop the posh girls bagging all the showers.

"I'll speak to Miss Gallacher after breakfast," she said. "She can sort it out with their teacher."

I envied someone with so little to worry about. As I drank my orange juice I couldn't help wondering – though without much conviction – whether last night's sightings of Piggy had been another Weerdwood dream.

After breakfast, we were told to clean our teeth, put on our jackets and meet in the courtyard in front of the house. It was parky out there, though my shivering wasn't entirely to do with the weather. In my fright over Piggy, I'd all but forgotten the bricked-up window above the front door. Now, although I deliberately stood with my back to it, my neck prickled and I thought I could feel its menacing stare. I was thankful when Rusty came bounding out and ordered us all round the corner into the flower garden. His good humour apparently restored, he looked us over casually, glanced at our medical notes on his clipboard and divided us into three groups of five.

"Red, green and orange," he grinned. "Nothing to do with the colour of your faces."

Of course this feeble joke sank like a lead balloon. Rusty was not a funny guy.

Unsurprisingly I was in orange – never my favourite colour. I could see at once that it was the weeds' group; the only other people in it from Underwood Academy were Willie Andrews, who looked like a pigeon on stilts, and Cameron Hornby, who was overweight and had a mysterious illness which prevented him from playing outdoor games in winter and doing anything he didn't want to do all the year round. As the red group (big and beefy and inevitably including Gillian) strode off into the wood with Rusty and the green group (ordinarily healthy and containing everyone else I knew well) departed with Mrs Finch and Miss Gallacher to the other side of the house, I was left standing on an overgrown path with two boys I thought were twits and two strange girls from Queen Maud's College. So much for my plan to keep close to people I knew.

The leader of the orange group was Rusty's assistant, Jess Brooks.

"We're going to do some clearing up in the flower garden," she told us briskly. "It should really have been done in the autumn, but we didn't find time. Now there's a rush to cut back dead foliage and make room for new growth. We're expecting our first group of disabled guests in July," she added, "so we want to have everything looking good for them."

The sky had the dull sheen of aluminium and a stiff, salty breeze was blowing from the firth. As Jess handed out shears and leather gloves and warned us cheerily not to cut off our fingers, Cameron said he wasn't feeling well and his mum would say he should lie down. Jess quelled him with a cold look. We spread out unsociably, even the posh girls seeming reluctant to talk to each other.

I don't know whether anyone reading this has ever tried to cut back a soggy, withered and horrendously overgrown herbaceous border, ten feet deep and about three hundred metres long. If not, you can take it from me that four puny teenagers (plus one saddo who'd rather have been in bed) impacted minimally on the job. Jess on her own hacked down more dead lupins and delphiniums in half an hour than the rest of us did all together. I had that horrible feeling when your body runs with sweat inside your clothes, while your hands and feet are numb with cold. I couldn't feel the shears through the thick leather gloves and I kept dropping them into my teeny pile of stems and leaves. As the wind soughed in the bare branches and rooks cawed raucously overhead, I kept a wary eye open for Piggy. Still he didn't show.

I suppose I'd been working for about an hour (although it seemed like twelve) before I had a pile of grot worth humping to the rubbish heap beside the half-derelict greenhouse at the end of the garden. It was a messy job and I had to take off my gloves to pick bits of dead leaf off my new navy-blue fleece. I was still standing by the rubbish heap when I saw a deerhound. I knew the breed because one of our neighbours in Gilmerton had one – an enormous, grey creature with an aristocratic face, shaggy coat and long, silvery legs. I thought he was cool, but Mum didn't like him because our spaniel Benjy went loco every time he pranced past our gate. The Weerdwood dog was scuffling in the loam under the beech trees beyond the lawn, tossing up flurries of brittle brown leaves. He seemed unaware of anyone in the garden, but when I whistled to him he pricked his ears and began to run eagerly towards me.

"Come on," I said, patting my knee encouragingly. "Good dog – come on."

The dog came on until he was a couple of metres away from me, then he changed his mind. Skidding to a halt on the wet grass, he splayed his feet and dropped his tail. To my alarm, I saw his hackles rise and his teeth gleam as he uttered a low, unfriendly growl. I was preparing to bolt when suddenly he swivelled and ran away among the trees.

Watching him go, I blew out my cheeks with relief. At

that moment, being attacked by an outsize dog was all I needed to turn me into a total gibbering wreck. As I pulled on my gloves and went back to work, however, I felt I had no one but myself to blame. We'd had Benjy for four years, and I should have known that dogs are suspicious of people whose smell they don't recognise. I reckoned the deerhound and I would get on fine when I knew his name, and could make friends with him in the presence of his owner. For of course the dog must belong to one of the Weerdwood adults. How else to explain the doggy sounds I'd heard outside my door last night?

5

A Family Face

At eleven o'clock, Jess called out that we'd break for half an hour.

"There'll be a snack ready in the dining-room," she told us. "You can eat it there, or bring it into the garden if you like."

I tagged along to the cloakroom with the two Queen Maud's College girls, but neither of them spoke, either to each other or to me. I'd been to the loo and was washing my hands when the door swung open and the girls from the red and green groups came barging in. They seemed to have connected more successfully than our group had; maybe digging a ditch and pruning apple-trees were better bonding activities than hacking at dead delphiniums. Gillian, red and sweaty and obviously having a great time, didn't even say "Hello". As I dried my hands I could hear her broad

Scots voice coming from a toilet cubicle, cutting through the refined English tones of her new mates.

"Have your feet dried out yet, Sybil? God, did you ever see anything like Rusty's face when the spade went through that water-pipe?"

Anne, Gemma and Lucy weren't much better.

"Oh, here's Con."

"Cheers, Con."

"Bye, Con."

I felt my face flushing, but I wouldn't let them see I cared. Pushing through the swing-door, I went back alone to the dining-room. There was still no sign of Piggy, so I helped myself to a Diet Coke and a cheese scone and carried them out through the glass door that opened from the adjacent sitting-room into the garden. I was sitting on a flight of stone steps, faking intense interest in a sundial mounted on a mossy carved pillar, when someone came and sat down beside me. To my surprise, I recognised one of the two Queen Maud's College girls who had also been assigned to the orange group.

"Hi," she said. "My name's Grace Kendrick. May I join you?"

"Of course. I'm Con Carberry," I replied, trying not to sound as grateful as I felt.

But of course, being me, I couldn't think of anything else to say. Glancing sideways, I could see Grace Kendrick looking me over. She had a beautiful face, broad at the cheekbones and narrow at the chin, with deep blue eyes and hair to die for, thick and curly and the colour of ripe wheat. I reckoned she was a couple of years older than me and somehow she reminded me of someone I'd seen before. On television? I really couldn't remember. I watched her flick crumbs of scone off her violet tracksuit and swig some coffee from a plastic cup.

"Enjoying yourself?" she asked teasingly.

"No," I said emphatically, and we both laughed.

"So why did you come?" Grace inquired.

I could hardly tell the whole truth, but what I said was accurate enough.

"It seemed like a fun idea, back in November when we got the info. I've never been away from home before, and I just thought it would be cool." Then, fearing that I'd sound babyish to a fifteen-year-old from boarding-school, I added hastily, "It's not that I'm homesick or anything. It's just that I don't like being in the wimpy group without any of my friends." Hardly tactful, as I immediately realised. Fortunately Grace didn't seem bothered, so I ventured to go on. "Why did you come?" I asked.

There was a little pause, while a chaffinch hopped onto the step and helped itself to crumbs of scone. I thought Grace wasn't going to answer, but eventually she said, "Oh, curiosity, really. My mother is descended from the old admiral who built this house."

"As in Admiral's Lodge," I said, amazed.

"That's the one," agreed Grace with a grin. "My mum is a great-niece of the Lord Weare who founded the Weerdwood Trust and left it the house to use as a youth centre. My parents work abroad – which is why I'm stuck at QM – and in the holidays I've never persuaded them to bring me this far north. So when the chance came to spend some time here, I jumped at it."

I could feel my eyes widening in astonishment, not only because I was fratting with someone with a title in her family. That she should be telling me this story seemed an almost spooky coincidence, given my inexplicable obsession with Weerdwood.

"So what do you think of it?" I asked, trying to sound offhand.

Grace wrinkled her nose in distaste.

"I absolutely hate it," she said. "The Admiral's Lodge bit is quite cosy, but the rest is sinister. I don't mean in the way that muttonhead was banging on about last night – I don't believe in ghosts as such. But this place has a scary atmosphere – sad and bad at the same time. I felt it the minute we got out of the bus last night. And that window above the door, patched like a wounded eye – it's gruesome. You wonder what on earth's behind it."

I had wondered too. Unfortunately, just as the conversation was becoming really fascinating, Jess came out of the dining-room with our fellow oranges in tow.

"Right, peeps. Back to work," she ordered. "Come on, Cameron and Willie. That means you too."

I expected Grace to go off with the other girl from her own school, but instead she walked with me across the spongy lawn. What she said next was really nice.

"Don't feel bad, Con. They always put me in the wimpy group too, because I had heart operations when I was a kid. I'm perfectly OK now, but I think teachers are scared I'll fall down dead and they'll be blamed. Do you have a problem?"

"Asthma when I was younger," I told her, adding curiously, "What's wrong with your friend?"

Grace looked puzzled.

"My friend?" she repeated. "Oh, you mean Isabelle. She isn't my friend and I don't think there's anything wrong with her. I suppose the Rusty creature just needed three groups of five. See you at lunch, then."

It was as damp and chilly as ever and none of my problems had gone away. But as I picked up my shears and pulled on my gloves, I felt better than I had since leaving the carpark in Perth twenty-four hours before.

By that evening, I'd relaxed amazingly. Piggy Gillanders hadn't shown, and I was close to convincing myself that he had been a delusion caused by extreme tiredness and over-excitement. At lunch and supper Grace had insisted that I should sit beside her and, since two of what she called the 'QM girls' were now sharing a table with Gillian and a guy called Kevin Williamson, I was spared bitchy remarks about cuddling up to posh people. I'd told Grace about Mum and Mark and Benjy and the deerhound in our street. The only slightly puzzling moment had been when I mentioned the dog I'd encountered in the Weerdwood garden.

"Oh? I didn't notice him," said Grace. "Isabelle, did you see a dog in the garden today?"

"No," replied Isabelle, shaking her auburn head.

I was surprised, since I'd been keeping a wary eye on the creature all afternoon as he prowled among the trees, his long nose to the ground as if he were trying to pick up some elusive scent.

"I thought he might belong to Rusty," I suggested, but Grace didn't think so.

"Not if the nearest dog we're likely to hear lives at the farm up the road," she pointed out.

She was right, of course. But before I had time to start worrying, she began telling me about the house where she'd been brought up in India and the creatures that lived in the garden — geckos and mongooses and parakeets and a shuddersome variety of snakes.

She made it really interesting, and by the time we slouched through to the sitting-room for our first evening's entertainment, I was feeling quite mellow. I sat between Gillian and Cameron, with Grace opposite in the chair where Piggy had — or hopefully had not — sat last night.

As soon as Rusty stood up to introduce the folk trio that had "kindly consented to entertain us", I knew Grace was going to spend the evening trying to make me laugh. It shouldn't have been difficult, because the folk group was dire; three weirdos with long limp hair and the kind of droopy tie-dye shirts my mum used to wear in the 1970s. One played a fiddle and one a wee harp called a clarsach, while the vocalist wailed as bitterly about the defeat of Bonnie Prince Charlie in 1746 as if it had happened yesterday.

> *"Although my heart is unco sair,*
> *And lies fu' lowly in its lair,*
> *Yet the last drap o' blude that's there*
> *I'll gie for bonny Charlie."*

Not cutting edge, exactly. So why wasn't I reduced to fits of giggles by Grace's teeth-gnashing and eye-rolling? Because, like a fuzzy image sharpening into focus, I had remembered where I'd seen her face before. It wasn't someone on television she'd reminded me of, nor anyone I'd actually seen. When I'd been wandering through Weerdwood in my dreams, there had been a portrait, hanging above a marble chimneypiece, of a young woman in a white dress. She'd been like the twin of Grace Kendrick, blue-eyed and golden-haired, with broad cheekbones and a wide, full mouth. *But that wasn't all.* At her side there had been a grey deerhound, so vividly painted you'd have thought he was going to leap out of the frame. He was identical to the one that couldn't belong to Rusty and had only been seen by me.

Suddenly I didn't want to stay downstairs any longer. While the folk trio packed up and the others drifted back to the dining-room for hot chocolate, I slipped away and went upstairs. If I'd had a room of my own, I'd have gone under the duvet and howled. But Anne and Gillian might come in at any moment, so I undressed and locked myself in the shower. As the hot water rained down over my body, I ordered myself to stop being such a fool. *Why shouldn't the faces be the same if people are related? The dog was just a coincidence – deerhounds are quite a common breed. There was some natural reason for the noises I heard in the corridor last night. Someone in the house must have a dog, for God's sake.*

As an explanation it had as many holes as a sieve, and I'd have had to be a worse fool than I was to believe it. Miserably I cleaned my teeth and blasted my short hair with the drier on the wall, then trailed back to my room. The air seemed stuffy, so I thought I'd open the window before getting into bed. It was as I parted the curtains that I heard dog noises – not in the corridor this time. In fact, the window was already open and, as I peered out into the cold, moonlit garden, I saw the deerhound sitting in the middle of the frost-crusted lawn. Like a grey ghost with his muzzle pointed to the sky, he was howling his loneliness and sadness to the moon. As I stood trembling, the sound faded and the creature dissolved like smoke before my eyes.

6

Sharing a Secret

It's amazing how seeing a ghost changes the scale of your terrors. I'd had a dreadful night, with spells of feverish tossing punctuated by horrible dreams. As I whimpered in the dark behind a bricked-up window or ran from hounds pursuing me through a tangled mesh of heather, Piggy Gillanders hadn't been uppermost in my mind. When I stumbled down, aching and sandy-eyed, to breakfast, and saw him standing in his apron behind the dining-room counter, I felt the familiar cold tightening of my stomach. But as I helped myself to cereal and sloshed milk over it, I realised that he was no longer the most terrifying thing I'd encountered at Weerdwood.

I suppose that was why, when at our mid-morning break I saw him coming across the lawn, I didn't do what I'd have done yesterday – run away screaming to find Miss

Gallacher. Grace had gone to the loo and the rest of our group was in the dining-room, but Jess was sitting on the steps drinking coffee with Mrs Finch, the bouncy but nice teacher from Queen Maud's College. They were well within earshot, and I thought – OK. It was bound to happen and I might as well get it over. I sat down quietly on a carved stone bench and Piggy sat down beside me. But as I watched him sucking his teeth and fiddling with his ear-studs, I couldn't help flinching and sidling away.

"Hurt me and I'll scream," I warned hoarsely.

"Oh, God!" Now it was Piggy flinching. "That's what I need to talk to you about. I'd have come yesterday, but it was my day off and I had to go to see my social worker in Inverness. I don't want to hurt you, Con. I've changed, honestly."

I couldn't restrain a sceptical snort.

"The last time you hurt me was at my dad's funeral," I reminded him bitterly. "You crushed my hand. *At my dad's funeral*. Why should I believe anything you say?"

I had turned my head away, but now I looked to see how he would respond. When I saw that I'd scored a point, I felt a fierce little glow of satisfaction.

"Con," he said, in a 'trust-me' voice that made me squirm, "I know I did evil things. I apologise for everything. But it was a long time ago. I've been in custody since then. Did you know that?"

"Yip," I nodded. "Your mum told mine."

"It was the best thing that ever happened to me," said Piggy, looking earnest. "Three years ago, I was on drugs and

37

completely out of control. I'd been excluded from school and I spent my time stealing to feed my habit. If I couldn't get smack I smashed things up and set fire to buildings. My mum couldn't handle me, and I couldn't handle myself.

"But in the detention centre my luck changed. I had sessions with a psychiatrist – a really good guy. He made me face up to the truth about myself, and showed me there was a better way. I got help to come off drugs and I got points for good behaviour, so instead of finishing my time I was released last year into the care of the Weerdwood Trust. They work with young offenders and gave me a job here. Of course it's conditional on me keeping off drugs and going straight, but I've managed so far. I'm studying for exams and I really want to do something useful with my life."

You have to admit it sounded good, if a bit self-obsessed. Did I believe him? Not a chance. I didn't think leopards could change their spots, and I certainly didn't think a single word of apology could wipe out the fear and mind-sickness this guy had caused me for three and a half years of my life.

"Why are you telling me this, Piggy?" I asked coldly.

He gave me an imploring look.

"Because I don't want you to tell the guys here how I used to frighten you," he said, "or give them the impression you're still scared of me. I'm on probation and – well, it wouldn't help my cred with Rusty Cooper. Please, Con, don't mess it up for me – and *please* don't call me Piggy. I'm not even called Drummond now. I've got a new name for a new life."

Heh, heh, heh, I wanted to say, but didn't. It was dawning on me that, for the first time in my long acquaintance with Piggy, I just might have a decent card in my hand. As Grace came out of the house and Jess rose from the steps, I got up too.

"All right," I said grudgingly. "Just keep away from me. Don't bug me, and I won't say anything. But if you threaten me, or try to hurt me –"

I could see relief in his eyes, but also disappointment as he realised I hadn't fallen for his reformed character act. As he stood up, he looked downcast and very tired.

"I won't hurt you ever again," he said.

I don't know why I said what I did. God knows, I didn't want to prolong the encounter. But as Piggy turned away towards the house, I heard myself blurt out, "That grey deerhound – who does it belong to?"

Was I hoping, even now, for reassurance? If so, I certainly didn't get it. Piggy's thin body jerked as if a bolt of electricity had gone through him. When he whipped round to face me, his eyes were stretched and his mouth trembling visibly.

"You've seen it," he gasped. "You – too –"

Then he fled, speeding between the tattered flowerbeds as if the phantom dog was snapping at his heels. That was when I knew why he looked like a skeleton covered with skin – and that I shared a secret with the last person on earth with whom I wanted to share anything.

"Do you know that guy Jake?" asked Grace, as we pulled on our gloves and prepared to get hacking again.

There didn't seem much point in denying it.

"We went to the same primary school," I explained, "before I moved to Edinburgh."

"What an amazing coincidence," said Grace predictably. But then she said something that nearly blew my mind. "He's quite a cutie, actually. Nice haircut and his studs are to die for. A bit like David Beckham, don't you think?"

I could hardly believe what I was hearing. That a fifteen-year-old was so starved for male company that she thought Piggy Gillanders was cute – let alone like David Beckham – was the best argument against single-sex education I had ever heard. I was opening my mouth to tell Grace exactly what I thought of her cutie, what he'd done and where he'd been for most of the last three years, when suddenly I remembered the pact I'd made with him only a few minutes earlier.

"Not my type," I muttered, as the grey dog came running through the trees.

7

Jake's Story

All that day and the next, the deerhound was never far
away from me. As I worked in the garden he circled among
the trees, sniffing and scuffling as if he was trying to find a
grave. Twice I saw him in the hall as I came indoors and
again I heard him scratching in the corridor after lights-out.
But when, during the night, I was shaken awake by bloodcurdling howls far closer than the farm up the road, Gillian
and Anne didn't even stir. Although the dog showed no
more interest in me, I was scared stiff. After the raging we'd
had from Rusty the first evening, however, I was afraid to
share my fears with anyone. The terrible thing was not
believing that anyone would back me up; I didn't trust Piggy
as far as I could kick him and it was plain that none of my
companions either saw or heard the dog.

Because I didn't know what else to do, I forced myself to

act normally. I joined in the usual girl-talk about hair products and fashion, swapped magazines and gossiped about pop stars. When a red Post Office van came up the drive, I joined the stampede into the hall. There was a letter for me from the friend who was looking after Benjy and a postcard from Mum and Mark, written at Glasgow Airport: "Missing you already . . . lots and lots of love . . ." Later Miss Gallacher gave me a copy of an e-mail from Lisbon: "Message for Con Carberry: We've arrived! Hotel wonderful, food and weather perfect. Hope you're having a great time."

The tragic thing was that I would have been having a great time, if my experience had been like everyone else's. After our stormy journey the weather had turned quiet, with mild, spring-like hours between the frosts of dawn and dusk. The great grey river flowed tranquilly against a backdrop of snow-capped mountains and even Weerdwood, seen from certain angles, evoked the dreamy, lightsome place it must once have been. Our work in the garden gradually began to make a difference, as the clearance of old growth revealed pale green shoots and crocuses unfolding in the light. And, as promised, there were other activities to vary our routine. One evening we played bingo, which was a howling success, the next we had dancing, which was less so. The imbalance of the sexes and our ages spelt doom; not even the QM girls were so starved for romance that they fancied smooching with Cameron and Willie.

The only thing I came close to enjoying was an outing on Thursday to a nearby community centre where we swam, and afterwards were allowed a free hour to explore the little fishing town of Poyntz. It was a faintly sunny, warmish day and, away from Weerdwood, I relaxed a little. Grace, who had decided that I was homesick and had taken me under her wing, stood me coffee and a slice of carrot cake in a tiny shop by the harbour. We bought some postcards and explored the narrow cobbled streets that clambered up the steep slope behind. I liked the elegant, lime-washed houses with their red roofs and tall chimneys. I enjoyed glimpses between them of fisher cottages with little fenced gardens, and silver flashes of sea.

"What a cool place," said Grace approvingly. "I wouldn't mind living here – having a cottage and a boat and going fishing in the bay. Maybe when I'm older, if I can afford it. I'm glad my family's shot of that creepy old Weerdwood, though."

Would this have been a good time to confide in her, to tell her that Weerdwood was even creepier than she imagined? As we walked back to the carpark by the harbour I was tempted, but somehow I couldn't get to the point. Sure, she'd said that Weerdwood had a bad atmosphere, but she'd also said she didn't believe in ghosts. I really liked her, and I certainly didn't want her looking at me as if I were some kind of kook.

As the minibus ran back along the coastal road, in the misty hour before nightfall by the sea, the tide was far out. Weedy rocks and banks of shingle were exposed, interwoven with braids of pale gold sand. The sky was pink like an oyster shell and I couldn't help enjoying its beauty – until I saw, splashing boisterously in the pools left by the tide, the grey deerhound. As Mrs Finch squeezed the bus between the narrow gateposts of Weerdwood, I looked out of the back window. Ghostly in the gathering dusk, the dog was padding along between the brown hedgerows, making for home. Words can't describe the terror and loneliness I felt.

I suppose it was only a matter of time before I had another conversation with Piggy – or Jake, as I must now call him, since keeping schtum about his nickname was part of the agreement between us. The only question was which of us would approach the other. I'd seen him watching me in the dining-room with something very like pleading in his dull, haunted eyes. But we'd avoided direct contact until we ran into each other in the hall on Friday, at the start of our first 'free afternoon'. You couldn't have said which of us communicated first. As Jake raised a questioning eyebrow, I nodded and said, "OK. Where?"

"In the garden," he said. "No sense in looking secretive. Besides, I'll be safer close to the house, where I can scream if you hit me."

I didn't know whether this was a joke or a jibe, so I ignored it.

"I'll get my jacket," I said.

Without giving myself time to think, I plucked my fleece from its peg in the cloakroom and went out through the glass door onto the terrace. Jake was sitting on the steps and, as I sat down beside him, I could see him watching the deerhound on the other side of the lawn.

"I'd kill that bloody animal," he growled, "if I didn't know it was dead already."

Of course, I knew this too, but it still chilled me to hear it said. I pulled up the zip of my fleece.

"How long have you been seeing it?" I asked.

Jake's fingers went to his ear-studs and he licked his lips nervously.

"Ever since I arrived," he said. "The first day I was here, Mary sent me into the kitchen garden to pick some beans. I saw the dog snuffling about on the drying green and I whistled to it."

"Did it come?"

"Yes and no. It pricked its ears and came running towards me, but when I put out my hand it changed its mind – snarled and ran away whining among the bushes."

"Same as me," I said. "I assumed it was real."

"Exactly," nodded Jake. "I wouldn't have thought anything of it, but when I mentioned it casually to Mary, she dropped the pot she was carrying. Then she said she'd never seen a dog at Weerdwood in her life."

"Do you believe her?"

Jake shrugged.

"I believe she hadn't seen that dog," he said. "Not many people have. But I don't believe she didn't know what I was talking about. She was certainly bothered enough to tell Rusty, because that night he came to see me in my room. Told me to keep my trap shut, because if the kids here thought there was a dog on the loose they'd start to panic. When I said surely they would see it without me pointing it out, he went ballistic. 'Don't get cocky with me, sonny,' I think was what he said. Then he jabbed his finger in my

45

chest and snarled that he didn't like troublemakers, and that if I caused him any grief he would have me back in the nick before my feet touched down. I couldn't see what all the fuss was about a damn dog. But of course I grovelled and promised not to mention it again. When you're in my position, you have to watch every step you take."

If I hadn't seen Rusty Cooper close to boiling over, I might have found this story harder to believe.

"So – you've been seeing the dog ever since?" I asked.

"Yip. In the garden, down on the shore, in the derelict part of the house. I've heard it howling in the night and heard it scratching in the passage outside my door. Twice it's jumped out on me in the yard and if I hadn't had something in my hand to throw at it, the brute would have been at my throat. Only last week I left a denim jacket on the bench outside the back door and when I came to pick it up it had been ripped to shreds."

I felt myself goggling with horror.

"But still you never told anyone?" I whispered.

Jake looked at me sadly.

"Con, you just don't get it," he said. "I'm only here as long as I keep out of trouble with Rusty. I don't like him, but he's my keeper and I have to accept that. If I can keep my nose clean for another six months, I've a good chance of a place at university. I won't do anything to risk that. I'd rather die than go back inside."

"OK, I see." I was silent for a moment, then I said, "On our first night, when Rusty was banging on about stupid idiots frightening other people – did he think you'd been blabbing?"

Jake laughed shortly.

"That would have suited him nicely," he said, "but luckily I had an alibi. I was down in Paisley with my social worker, visiting my mum. I only heard what happened from the guy who was helping out in the kitchen while I was away. There had been a group of Cub Scouts here on an adventure holiday. A wee laddie came to his leader in hysterics, howling that a big dog had bared its teeth at him then disappeared through a wall. That was the cue for all the other kids to start throwing wobblies and screaming that they'd seen ghosts too – headless ladies, turnip lanterns, things in white sheets, a whole bloody Hallowe'en parade. The rest of the visit was a disaster and their leaders were so fed up they took them home early.

"Our Rusty wasn't a happy boy. This place got off to a bad start. Not long after it opened – and to be fair, before Rusty took over – a young woman was drowned in the quicksand down at Sutor Point. It was on the telly and all over the newspapers. The adults were cleared of negligence, but a youth centre needs that kind of publicity like a hole in the head. If it gets around that kids are seeing spooks here, the whole enterprise is doomed. The Weerdwood Trust and the Government have pumped a colossal amount of money into this god-awful dump, and it's Rusty's head that'll roll if it all goes pear-shaped. That's why he's shit-scared. He can see Weerdwood going down the plug and him getting blamed."

I sat for a moment or two in the fragile March sunshine, twisting my silver bracelets round and round my wrist. As an explanation of Rusty's strange behaviour, Jake's story certainly hung together. But –

"Why us?" I asked eventually.

Jake shook his head.

"God only knows," he replied wearily.

He was right and I changed the subject.

"Jake," I said, remembering just in time not to call him Piggy, "the window of the room above the front door – why is it bricked up?"

I saw him repress a shudder.

"Someone died in there," he said, "away back before World War I. Mary told me, though she doesn't know the details. The owner of the house was so upset that he couldn't bear to go in again. He had the room sealed up and it's been like that for nearly a century. The door has big padlocks and wooden battens nailed all over it. Funny you should mention it, because I only heard this morning that it's to be opened up next week, in the latest stage of the restoration. More horrors to look forward to, I suppose."

This news was so shocking that my tongue jammed itself against the roof of my mouth. Before I could loosen it, Jake had got to his feet.

"Must go – I've got the potatoes to peel," he said.

I went on sitting on the step, feeling cold damp seeping through my trousers and numbing my behind.

Two weeks today, I'll be going home, I thought, trying to comfort myself – as if just then two weeks didn't seem like a hundred years.

8

Three of Us

I just hope no one imagines that this was the start of some big love-in between Jake Gillanders and me. We both carried far too much emotional baggage – an uneasy mix of guilt and self-interest on his part and resentment on mine – just to let the past fade away. But of course I had teasing to put up with from those who'd seen us together on the steps.

"Ha, ha, Con's got a new squeeze!"

"Yeah, we saw you. What'll your mum say?"

"When are you getting your ear-studs, Con?"

It was Lucy's wit that killed you.

"He is not my squeeze. We went to the same primary school," I said coldly.

"Well! Lucky old you!"

This response really mystified me. I already knew that Grace, who seemed to have good taste in other ways, thought that Jake Gillanders was Weerdwood's answer to football's finest. Now it seemed that Gillian, Gemma and Anne were also drooling over a guy who only needed some hair-dye and black eyeliner to turn him into a Goth. Had past experience made me blind to his sex-appeal? Don't make me laugh.

Actually, over the weekend, I rarely set eyes on Jake. He was working behind the scenes on Friday night and on Saturday we were away with Miss Gallacher and Mrs Finch to ten-pin bowling and the cinema in Inverness. On Sunday those of us who wanted to went to church in Poyntz. I went partly to get away from Weerdwood, and partly because I believe in God and I had a lot to pray about. I was glad I'd gone, because I liked the church with its high pulpit like the prow of a ship and clear glass windows through which you could see tombstones listing like grey boats in a sea of windblown grass. There was a smell of damp bibles and ancient dust, and during the sermon I passed the time by studying the marble memorials crowding the walls:

SACRED TO THE MEMORY OF
JOHN RAMSAY WALTER, 1st EARL WEARE
ADMIRAL OF HIS MAJESTY'S FLEET
KILLED BY NATIVES IN THE WEST INDIES
12 APRIL 1781
IN THE 49th YEAR OF HIS AGE

IN LOVING MEMORY OF
LIEUT. THE HON. PETER WEARE R.N.
WHO DIED AT THE BATTLE OF JUTLAND
1 JUNE 1916
AGED 20 YEARS

The inscriptions made depressing reading. The Weares had been a naval family with a terrible record of sudden and violent death. The youngest to perish at sea had only been fifteen, and I noticed that most of the women mentioned had died before they were thirty. I wondered if it was their ill luck that made their house feel so iffy.

When I did see Jake in the dining-room later on, however, I knew he was making an effort. He'd say something like, "Hi, Con. Have some of this macaroni cheese. It's Mary's speciality," or, "Try the cauliflower soup – it really hits the spot."

Maybe I should have responded more warmly, but horrible flashbacks prevented me. I'd see him throwing my teddy up into a tree and laughing at my distress. I'd see him grabbing the plastic sack with a goldfish I'd won at the fair and tipping it down a drain in Killoch Road. I'd see him dangling a worm in front of my nose and threatening to make me eat it. So I can't explain the impulse that made me hang back, when he was wiping down the counter after supper, and ask, "How's your mum, by the way? My mum would like to know."

"Not bad, thanks for asking," Jake replied. "She's moved to a flat at Anchor Mills and she's got a new boyfriend, so she's OK, I suppose."

"That's nice," I said. "It must have been hard for her, your dad leaving the way he did."

Jake paused with the sponge in his hand and eyed me incredulously.

"Oh, get real, Con," he groaned. "That vicious little ape wasn't my dad! I've no idea who my dad was, I had so many."

Talk about embarrassed! I didn't know where to look.

51

I didn't see much of the dog during the weekend either – only enough to remind me that it hadn't gone away. But every time I came back from an outing, I had to pass under the bricked-up window into the dingy, cobwebbed entrance hall.

"Jake says that next week they're going to open up the room behind that window," I told Gillian, who had been to church with me. "It hasn't been opened for nearly a century."

Gillian's eyes widened.

"Wow! Fantastic," she said with relish. "I hope we're allowed to be there when they open the door. Maybe there'll be bats, or a ghost saying, '*Woo-oo-oo!*'."

At moments like this, I wondered whether my friendship with Gillian could survive another two weeks of living cheek by jowl. I could think of nothing more repulsive than the opening of such a place. Before we had official news of it, however, something entirely unforeseen occurred.

Sunday had been another mild day, and the good weather held into the start of the new week. On Monday morning, the Post Office van came after breakfast and, as I took Mum's postcard from the table in the hall, I saw Grace pick up a striped air-mail envelope. She ran upstairs with it and I went into the dining-room to read my card. When the orange group assembled in the garden twenty minutes later, Grace wasn't there.

"Anyone know where she is?" asked Jess, as she handed out trowels. "Isabelle?"

Isabelle gave one of her languid shrugs.

"No, sorry."

"She got a letter from abroad this morning," I said, adding anxiously, "I hope it wasn't bad news."

Like all the adults, Jess took our welfare seriously.

"Go and see if you can find her, Con," she said. "If there's anything I can help with, come and fetch me."

Leaving my trowel by the path, I hurried indoors. After a quick squint into the empty sitting-room, I ran upstairs to the room Grace shared with two of the other QM girls. When I'd tapped and got no response, I opened the door a crack and squinted in. Grace was sitting huddled on the side of her bed with the letter crumpled on the floor at her feet. Her nose was red and her eyes puffy with crying.

"What's the matter, Grace?" I asked in alarm, hurrying to sit beside her. "Has something bad happened at home?"

"No!" I knew from the way Grace scowled and bared her teeth that her tears were of anger as well as grief. "My mum and dad are in their usual good health. They've been to see tigers in Bangladesh and the new hospital at Udhampur is going like a fair. Normally I'm supposed to know these things by telepathy. They don't e-mail me, they hardly ever write a letter, and they take no interest in me from one year's end to the next. But just let me do something off my own bat and they're down on me like a ton of bricks. Parents! Who needs them?"

This was strong stuff, and fascinating to someone who had always thought posh people spoilt and over-privileged.

"Do you want to tell me about it?" I asked.

For a moment Grace looked unsure, but then it all came tumbling out.

"OK. Normally at QM you have to get your parents'

permission before you spend time out of school, but because mine are always on the move and normally couldn't care less where I am – provided I'm not interfering with their mission to save the world – my consent forms are signed by my UK guardian, our family solicitor Mr Hartnoll."

I was out of my depth already.

"How do you mean – save the world?" I asked.

Grace made a rude face.

"My grandfather," she explained, "made a fortune from distilling whisky. My father inherited a disgusting amount of money and my mother has the Weares' passion for giving it away. They run a charity that builds hospitals in remote parts of India. Nothing wrong in that, but they're obsessive do-gooders and people like them really shouldn't have a child. Mum brought me back to the UK from India to have my last heart operation when I was seven. As soon as she knew it had been successful, she parked me at boarding-school and went abroad again. QM's a good school academically and I have plenty of cash, but in the last eight years I've only been with my parents eleven times. It didn't even occur to me to ask them about Weerdwood. The annoying thing is that if old Hartnoll hadn't been writing to them about something else and spilled the beans, they'd never have known I was here."

I was deeply shocked. I'd often thought I'd had a difficult childhood, but compared with Grace's and, come to think of it, Jake's, it had been positively rosy. Mum loved me, I was best friends with Mark, and my own dad, before illness changed him, had always been there for me. I glanced cautiously at Grace.

"So – what's upset you particularly?" I asked.

Grace kicked the crumpled paper at her feet.

"This morning," she said tightly, "I got this letter from my mum – the first I've had for two months. She's gone absolutely ape. She says I had no business to come to Weerdwood without asking her permission, which she would never have given. Says it's a horrible house where dreadful things have happened, and it should have been razed to the ground years ago. Orders me not to go anywhere alone, and says if I see a ghost it'll be no one's fault but my own."

It was one of those times when you feel you should say something, but the right words don't come. I heard myself mumbling, "I – um, well, *actually*," but Grace didn't pause.

"The worst of it is," she said, "that she's right, Con. You know I've had bad vibes here from the beginning, and –" she sucked her lips nervously "– now I have seen a ghost. Remember one night you asked me if I'd noticed a grey dog in the garden?" I nodded gravely. "I hadn't then," continued Grace, "but I saw it yesterday when you were at church. I whistled to it and it came bounding towards me, but when it got scent of me it growled and sidled away. It was awful – I could hear the poor thing crying in the wood as if it was heartbroken. Isabelle and Emily were right beside me on the terrace, but when I said, 'I wonder who that dog belongs to?' they said, 'What dog?' and looked at me as if I was loopy. But you've seen it, haven't you, Con?"

"Yes," I told her, "and Jake has too. So there are three of us now."

9

Breakthrough

The weather that day was again fine, but Jess said a change was coming and she was right. In the late afternoon dark clouds approached Weerdwood from the west and, while we were at supper, the first raindrops bounced on the terrace outside the dining-room. Awake in the night, I heard wind whooshing through the trees and rain spattering like grit on the window. When we got up on Tuesday morning it was bucketing so hard that pools were forming on the lawn and the estuary had disappeared behind a wall of fog. I'd hardly slept and, as I dragged myself down to breakfast, I was so wired I could have screamed.

No prizes, of course, for guessing what had kept me awake. All night long the deerhound had been howling like a lost soul, his eerie cries counterpointing the wind. The knowledge that there were two other people in the house who could hear him was no comfort, since I spent the wakeful hours fearful that, due to my big mouth, a relationship was taking off between them.

After I'd told Grace that Jake and I had both seen the dog, she'd looked thoughtful, but all she'd said was, "I suppose we'd better go down now." She'd washed her face, gone to the loo and accompanied me out into the garden. "We'll talk again later," she'd promised as she picked up her trowel, but the day went by without that happening. Grace had been very quiet, choosing to weed along the orchard wall at the far end of the garden, following a shaft of weak sunlight as it moved across the rough grey stone. I didn't intrude, but I couldn't help watching her as the deerhound jinked restlessly among the trees. She kept looking at it, then trying to turn away.

At four o'clock, as I was knocking mud off my wellies before going indoors, I saw two things that disturbed me. A builder's truck was parked in the courtyard, and two men in dungarees were unloading pickaxes, bags of cement and a new sash window, carefully wrapped in a clear plastic sheet. Jake, armed with a large brush, was sweeping up the contents of a cement bag that had burst as it hit the ground. To my amazement – and yes, to my annoyance – I saw Grace go up to him and tap him on the arm. I don't know how long they talked, because just then Miss Gallacher called me to give me another e-mail and I had to go into the house.

I suppose you could say it was none of my business. Grace and Jake were both older than me and if they wanted to talk privately, so what? You could also say I was jealous, but that wasn't the right word. Sure, I was miffed that Grace had talked to Jake alone – I was the one who'd tried to help her and now I felt excluded. But you can only be jealous if someone has something you want, and God knows I didn't want Jake Gillanders. What troubled me most was that Grace, who had made no secret of liking Jake, didn't know the person she was cosying up to. OK, perhaps he did appeal to her. There's no accounting for taste. But he was a guy with a hellish record of physical and psychological bullying, he'd been on drugs and in detention for a serious offence, and I didn't believe his remorse was worth a hill of beans.

Which was the crunch, really. I thought that if Grace was going to start something with Jake she ought to know the truth, but I was too chicken to tell her. Of course I told myself piously that it would be wrong to break my promise not to reveal Jake's past. But in fact I was scared stiff that, if I warned Grace and he found out, he'd be waiting for me round every corner, scowling and whispering the threats that were worse than actual blows. By the time I got down to breakfast on Tuesday morning, I'd worked myself into such a lather I couldn't go near him. Foregoing my bacon roll, I took some cereal and went to sit alone at a corner table.

I'd only been there for a couple of minutes when Grace joined me with some toast and orange juice. This was unusual, as the QM girls usually breakfasted together in total silence; Grace said that at boarding-school no one ever spoke to anyone else before ten. She was as white as a sheet and smudgy about the eyes, and I reckoned she hadn't slept much either.

"I'm sorry – I meant to speak to you last night," she said. "Only at supper I couldn't shake off Finchy, then I couldn't get near you at that stupid beetle drive. I wanted to tell you I've spoken to Jake. I suggested that, since we seem to be the only ones haunted, the three of us should get together and see if we can work out what the hell's going on here. There must be some reason, after all. "

I suppose I was mollified, though my moral problem remained unresolved.

"What did he say?" I asked curiously.

"Oh, he shilly-shallied a bit saying it would be difficult, since he doesn't have much time off. Then he asked me if you had told me anything about him, and I said only that you'd once gone to the same school. We talked a bit more, and eventually he said he'd be free this afternoon between four and five-thirty, which fortunately is our chill-out time too. We're to be in the sitting-room and he'll pass by casually and stop to speak to us."

Knowing a fix-up when I saw one, I didn't bother to reply. Grace fetched us some coffee and we drank it, never thinking that before four o'clock yet another weird phenomenon would have invaded our haunted world.

If anything, the storm outside had thickened since breakfast began. When Rusty got up and banged on the table for attention, the terrace was awash and the wind was gusting against the house, making the windows rattle.

"No outdoor work today," he said, "unfortunately, since you've all been doing so well. But never mind. We've three bedrooms upstairs ready for painting – overalls provided and no experience required. Everyone in the hall at half eight, please – oh, and one other thing." He paused, giving us the smile that lifted his bearded lip above his teeth, but never touched his eyes. "We'll be having the builders in today, opening the room above the front door. It's a bit of a mystery, that room – all we know for sure is that it hasn't been opened for close on ninety years. We've no idea what, if anything, is in there, but it's bound to be interesting. Suppose we alert you when the door's ready to be opened? Then anyone who wants to witness a moment in Weerdwood's history can come and have a look."

"I really wonder about that guy," muttered Grace, but I didn't respond. Across the dining-room I had caught the eye of Jake, who was stacking dirty plates behind the serving counter. His face was like chalk and, for the first time ever, a wave of sympathy passed between us.

No help for it, though – we had to obey orders. At half-past eight I was climbing the elegant but filthy stair, then passing through the empty drawing-room with the tattered peacock wallpaper and marble fireplace that I knew so well from my dreams. I could even see the dark rectangle on the wall where the portrait of the young woman who looked like Grace had hung, and the hooks left there when it had been taken down. Was I surprised? No, I'd have been surprised if it had been different. Beyond the drawing-room was a dingy landing with a creaky wooden floor and doors on three sides. Most were open, giving glimpses of rooms full of ladders, dust-sheets and big tins of paint. Only one, as Jake had said, was barred by three heavy battens nailed diagonally across it. Gillian nudged me.

"*Woo-oo-oo!*" she said.

"Oh, do shut up," snapped Grace, saving me the trouble.

In other circumstances it would have been good fun, sloshing sunny yellow emulsion paint onto the walls of a room overlooking the orchard and the river. It was Jess's day off, so Rusty and Mrs Finch were in charge of the orange group. They went up ladders and did the high bits while we messed about below with brushes, rollers and paint trays. Cameron and Willie had a cool time, getting more paint on themselves than they did on the walls. Grace and Isabelle who, like all the QM girls, were at Weerdwood to collect points for a Duke of Edinburgh's award, worked doggedly. I tried to concentrate on getting a clean line between the wall and the skirting-board. But my ears were pricked for the sound of the builders arriving and when, about half-past ten, I heard boots clumping across the drawing-room and men's voices outside, I wondered if I would pass out with the tension of it all.

Actually, we had been downstairs and had our elevenses before there was any sign of activity, and it was nearly midday when Miss Gallacher stuck her head round the door and said, "They're ready, if anyone wants to look."

I didn't want to look and Grace didn't either, but there's a strange momentum on such occasions. As the others, jostling excitedly, emerged onto the landing, we were swept along with them. It seemed everyone in the house had come. Jess was still in her pyjamas and Mary had come up from the kitchen, pulling a tense and very reluctant Jake.

"He's afraid of ghosts," said Mary cruelly, and everyone apart from Grace and me laughed.

Scared but fascinated, I watched a young guy in dungarees prop the three battens against the wall. An older man, holding a large flashlight in his left hand, turned the doorknob with his right. The door grated on its hinges, then stuck in grot on the floor. The workman put his shoulder to it and heaved. There was a rasping sound as it suddenly gave way. Gillian uttered a high-pitched giggle – *and someone came out*. What I *saw* was a faceless figure wrapped in smoke, drifting through the dark aperture before folding and wafting away. What I *felt* was that some strong and malevolent force had escaped from the bricked-up room and was now on the loose. Grace's hand clutched mine – whether to comfort herself or to comfort me, I didn't know.

Now everyone was moving towards the open door and I was carried forward in the press. The workman shone his flashlight into the pitch-dark room and, unable to help myself, I looked. I had never seen anything so creepy in my life and I pray to God I never do again. The whole place was swathed in grey cobwebs and overlaid by a pale epidermis of dust. There was a bed, its pillows and quilt nibbled by mice but otherwise undisturbed since it was made up nearly a century ago. There were curtains, torn and furry like moleskin, hanging before the blind, broken window. There was a dressing-table with a blackened mirror and a small piano, its crumbling keys exposed and tatters of music still hanging on the stand. And there was a smell so mouldy and revolting that even the unhaunted recoiled in disgust. I thought I was going to be sick, but it was Jake who suddenly made a retching noise, clapped his hand over his mouth and bolted back into the drawing-room.

There was total silence as Rusty stepped forward and closed the door.

10

What Grace Saw

I know it's rude to eavesdrop on purpose, but, if people leave
the door ajar and are hollering at the pitch of their lungs, you
can't be blamed for overhearing. At four o'clock, leaving the
other girls chilling out on their beds, Grace and I went
downstairs for our 'casual' meeting with Jake. I hadn't been
able to speak to Grace privately since the opening of the
mysterious room, and I was hoping we'd have a few quiet
moments alone to exchange impressions. No chance of that,
however. Rusty and Jess were in Rusty's office, which was
next to the sitting-room. The door was off the latch and they
were going at each other like two cats in hell. Hear them in
the sitting-room? You could have heard them in Australia.

Embarrassed, I raised my eyebrows at Grace, but she
merely shrugged and dropped into an armchair. All the posh
girls treated Admiral's Lodge like a hotel and secretly I

admired their style. I sat down too and pretended to read a magazine, but I was really only interested in the row raging next door.

"You're a fool, Rusty," Jess was snarling. "This is your second big mistake in less than a week. First you put the idea into the kids' heads that this place is haunted, then you actually invite them to look into that chamber of horrors upstairs. It shouldn't have been opened up when we had a group here, and certainly not when they were working a few yards away. There'll be complaints, you'll see."

"Oh, for God's sake, Jess!" There was a thump as Rusty's fist hit the table. "Can't you understand? These are not infants, they're young adults. It's far better they get an official version from us than go listening to old wives' tales in Poyntz General Store. That's what happened with that stupid little Cub Scout, or have you forgotten?"

"No, I haven't. That was a one-off. What I'm saying –"

"Shut up, and listen for once." Rusty was practically spitting teeth. "Of course I'd have preferred to have the builders when the house was empty, but I have to take these guys when I can get them. I also have to take groups when I can get them, with the Weerdwood Trust always breathing down my neck about accountability. If a lift is to go through the floor of that damned room before the first disabled kids arrive, I have to get it cleared out and the window mended smartish. I know you think you could do my job better –"

"Do your job better?" screeched Jess. "Right now, anyone could do your job better. Anyone who could see that kids shouldn't have been there when that ghastly place was opened. Did you see their faces? It's a wonder only one of them threw up."

"Give me strength!" Rusty groaned. "Do you think I wanted them gawping either? If the good weather had held just one more day, it needn't have happened. But they had to work indoors and painting upstairs is what needs doing right now. Wasn't it better to invite them all than to have one or two peeking and spreading rumours worse than the reality? It's only a bedroom, for God's sake. I want openness here —"

Jess's scornful laughter tore through Rusty's words.

"*Openness? You?* I won't listen to any more of this."

"Thank God for that. Why don't you apply for a transfer?"

"Why don't I? I often wonder."

I don't think Jess even noticed Grace and me when she crashed out of the office, slamming the door behind her. Her hair was ruffled, her dark face disfigured by a scowl. The silence seemed deafening when she'd gone.

"Happy days," I said.

"Yeah. Lovely people," murmured Grace.

It was nearly half-past four when Jake poked his head into the sitting-room. I guessed he'd been skulking nearby, waiting for the storm to subside before venturing to join us.

"Is the coast clear?" he asked nervously.

"Yes, the Fury has departed," replied Grace. "Does this happen often?"

Jake was looking wrecked, but he grinned as he coiled his long body into a chair.

"Mary calls it 'a difference in management styles'," he said. "The laugh is that Jess and Rusty are engaged to be married.

Either they're screaming and tearing each other's hair out, or else they're giggling and pinching each other's bottoms. As long as they don't ask me to be a bridesmaid . . ."

I was intrigued. I like 'human interest' stories and, after the stressful day I'd spent, a little normal gossip would have hit the spot nicely. But Grace said sharply, "For heaven's sake! Haven't we more important things to discuss than nerds and their stupid romances? I thought all we had to work out is why the three of us keep seeing and hearing that damned deerhound, but now I reckon we've more to worry about. These twits upstairs have nothing to say but 'Eek!' and 'Bleu-gh!' and 'Yuk, what a sick-making smell!'. But Con was practically wetting her knickers when the door opened and you actually were sick, Jake. Why was that?"

I was shaken as much by her stroppy tone as by the insult. I'd never have guessed Grace could be so horrible. I thought she was taking a risk with Jake, but he didn't bridle. He glanced at me, then looked at Grace intensely with his pale blue eyes.

"I was sick," he said, "because when the door opened something abnormal came out. Something as invisible as the smell, but likely to hang around a lot longer."

Grace's eyelids flickered, but all she said was, "And you, Con?"

A cold finger seemed to touch my heart.

"I did see something," I managed to say. "A sort of grey, smoky figure. I wasn't wetting my knickers, actually, but I agree with Jake. Something escaped and I was sc-sc-scared." To my horror, I felt my eyes filling with tears, and I began to sob uncontrollably. "I don't like it here. I want to go home," I wailed.

Through my tears, I saw Jake stiffen, embarrassed by feminine emotion. Mumbling, "Sorry, see you later," he slid out of his chair and fled.

For an instant, I thought Grace was going to slap my face. She didn't, but I shrank from the fury in her eyes.

"Stop that at once," she hissed. "How dare you be so selfish? Don't you think I'd like to go home too, if I had a home to go to? Jake would like to go, but he can't because he'd be straight back behind bars. Oh, yes, yes," she added contemptuously, as I started in surprise. "He told me all about that yesterday, and about how he'd been rotten to you when you were a kid. Wah-wah, a bad boy stole your teddy, but now it's time you grew up. If we have to stay here and see this thing through, why the hell shouldn't you?"

There's nothing like indignation for drying your tears. I had never felt so belittled and insulted in my life.

"You may have a title in your family, Grace Kendrick, but you have no manners," I said bitterly. "Don't ever speak to me again."

I went out into the garden. It was piercingly cold and soon I was shivering in my light cardigan and indoor shoes, but it was the only place I could be sure of being alone. Huddled in the lee of the old sundial, I watched ragged clouds racing across the vast, treebound sky. *I'll pretend I'm ill, and go to Auntie Morag's*, I thought. *Even that would be better than this.*

Eventually the cold drove me indoors, and I had no choice

but to go upstairs, have a shower and get ready for the evening. I sat through supper but I couldn't eat and, when Jess announced that we were going to have a karaoke session, I knew I'd reached my limit. Miss Gallacher was spending the evening with friends in Inverness, so I went to Mrs Finch instead.

"My head aches and I have a sore tummy," I told her, not untruthfully.

To my surprise, since she seemed such a hearty, no-nonsense person, she was a lot more sympathetic than Miss Gallacher.

"Are you homesick, my love?" she asked, touching my cheek with her forefinger. Probably, teaching in a boarding-school, she knew the signs, but, on the day I'd been told it was time I grew up, I wouldn't admit it. "Have your periods started?" she asked next.

"Yes, but I don't think it's that," I said.

"Then I think an early night's the best idea," said Mrs Finch. "Get into bed and I'll come up later and give you some Milk of Magnesia. Before you go, though, you can tell me something. What's karaoke?"

When I'd explained, the expression of horror on her face was so comical that I couldn't help laughing. The thought of Mrs Finch aping Björk was about as funny as it could get. Upstairs alone, however, with only the wind and the distant thud of the karaoke machine to break the silence, my amusement quickly gave way to depression and fear. I tried to read for a while, but my ears were alert for the noise of the phantom dog and, although I was expecting Mrs Finch, when I heard a tap on the door I nearly jumped out of my skin. I was outraged when the handle turned and Grace Kendrick put her head into the room.

"Push off," I said violently. "I told you – I don't ever want to speak to you again." She came in anyway and plonked herself down on the end of my bed. I eyed her angrily over the edge of the duvet, envying her beautiful hair, perfect skin and cornflower eyes. Even in her mauve school shirt she looked like a model. "Are you deaf?" I inquired coldly.

Grace shook her head.

"Oh, Con," she said contritely, "I don't blame you for being angry, but please, please forgive me. I'm so ashamed. I don't know what happened this afternoon. I've never behaved so badly before in my life and I didn't mean a word of what I said. Jake did tell me yesterday about himself – he said that if we were going to have anything to do with each other, I should know where he was coming from. He said he was an absolute pig to you when you were a little kid. He thinks he was brutalised by his mother's boyfriend knocking him about, and he was jealous because you had such good parents. But he says he's really sorry – and grateful to you for not telling anybody here how much he scared you."

I gave her a sour, sceptical look. Grace sighed.

"Well, that's between the two of you," she said. "I'm here to apologise. I shouldn't have said what I did about your teddy, as if I thought a little kid being bullied was no big deal. And I shouldn't have shouted at you for crying. God knows, I'm frightened enough myself. Oh, *please*, Con." She reached out and touched my hand imploringly. "You're the only friend I have here apart from Finchy and I can hardly confide in her. You see –" she swallowed audibly "– I haven't told you what I saw coming out of that awful room this morning."

My anger melted as I looked into her beseeching blue eyes.

"OK. What did you see?" I asked gently.

"I saw myself," Grace said.

Momentarily, there was silence. Grace looked as if she couldn't believe what she'd just said, and I'm sure I looked as if I couldn't either. Eventually, sitting bolt upright, I heard myself say stupidly, "Sorry – how do you mean?"

Grace made a helpless gesture with her long hands.

"When the door was opened," she said, "I saw a sort of shadow too. Only then it took shape on the darkness, like a photograph in a developing dish. It was a fair young woman in a long white dress patterned with roses. I only saw her for a moment, but she definitely had my face. Oh God, Con, what's happening to me? I've never believed in ghosts and now I can't stop seeing them."

Of course, I had seen that young woman too, if not as a ghost, certainly as a dream. Perhaps, I thought with a twinge of guilt, I should have come clean with Grace earlier, but I'd stupidly convinced myself that the resemblance was natural. But before I could even begin to tell my story, the door opened and Mrs Finch came in with her bottle of Milk of Magnesia. A breath of kindly normality seemed to waft in with her.

"Oh, Grace, you're here. That's nice," she said placidly. "Hiding, are you?"

Grace smiled faintly.

"I don't think karaoke's my thing," she said.

"No? Then you'll be glad to hear it's nearly over. Gillian is singing something called *Like a Virgin* and I think that will be a hard act to follow. You get off to bed then, dear, unless you'd like some Milk of Magnesia too."

"No, thank you, Mrs Finch," said Grace, rolling her eyes behind her teacher's back as she opened the door. "Goodnight, Con. We'll talk tomorrow."

Mrs Finch measured out a dose of medicine and stuck the spoon in my mouth.

"It isn't easy, being away from home for the first time," she said. "I remember going to Guide camp when I was twelve and blubbing every night. Fortunately, it's never so bad again." She waited till I lay down and tucked the duvet round me. "I'm glad you and Grace have become friendly," she added. "She's a lonely girl and I don't think boarding-school suits her. Well, goodnight, my dear. Come to Room 7 if you need me."

I'd have swapped Miss Gallacher for Mrs Finch any day. But as I lay with the duvet pulled over my head, waiting for Gillian and Anne to crash in, my hope of retreating to Auntie Morag's faded. Once you know that someone else is depending on you, running scared stops being an option.

11

At Sutor Point

Perhaps the most tiresome thing about life at Weerdwood (other than seeing ghosts) was the near impossibility of ever having a private conversation. Every moment of the day was organised. Upstairs I couldn't turn round without falling over Gillian or Anne, while in the orange group I couldn't snatch two words with Grace before Cameron or Willie came butting in. These sad no-hopers actually fancied their chances with Grace, proving there's one born every minute. That was why, as I drifted thankfully into sleep, I wouldn't have bet on the probability of Grace and me having an uninterrupted chat next day. There was, however, to be an unexpected change in our routine.

Surprisingly, since a wet day in Scotland usually signals a wet spell, the day of plashing rain was only a weather blip. While I slept the deep sleep of the truly exhausted, the cloud rolled out to sea and the sun rose on another serene spring day.

"Great. We'll get the new water-pipe laid today," enthused Gillian, who was becoming a drains and ditches bore. As so often, she was over-optimistic. When we got downstairs, we could see from the dining-room window that the garden was still waterlogged; the beds were a sea of mud and every dip in the lawn was filled with a shimmering pool. Although I was feeling stronger after sleep, the thought of spending another day painting upstairs made my heart sink. I didn't even want to pass the door of the mysterious room and I was afraid of ever looking into it again. So I felt deep relief when Rusty got up to give us our instructions for the day.

"Since the garden needs another twenty-four hours to drain and you did so much painting yesterday," he said, "we've decided to give you an extra holiday today. Mrs Finch and Miss Gallacher will take us in the minibuses to Cromar Head, then Jess and I will walk you back by the shore path to Sutor Point. Lunch will be a barbecue on the beach and in the afternoon we'll go swimming at Poyntz Community Centre."

There was a buzz of approval, although I don't think anyone was totally fooled. We could hear the builders already banging about upstairs. It was hard not to suppose that the adults had decided to remove us from the scene while the room above the front door was stripped of its macabre furnishings. This was confirmed when Rusty added, "Half-past nine at the front door, please. Wear warm clothes and comfortable footwear, and bring a waterproof just in case. Oh, and bring your swimming bags too. You can leave them in the minibuses, then we won't have to come back here after lunch."

When we'd first arrived at Weerdwood, I don't think anyone would have predicted that the Underwood Academy crowd and the QM girls would ever have a word to say to each other. Perhaps being thrown together to work and play had forced the two groups to jell. Certainly it now seemed quite natural for Gillian, Willie and me to travel in the QM minibus with Grace, Isabelle and Emily, while the other QM girls cheerfully scrambled into ours. Cameron had said that the walk would be too tiring for him, so Rusty had sent him off to help Mary and Jake. It was clear from the grin on Willie's face that he thought this would give him a clear run with Grace – as if. The change from smiley face to sad face was instant as he tried to sit beside her and she heaved him off the seat.

"Push off and stay off," she growled.

Maybe 'jell' was too strong a word.

I took Willie's place beside Grace, but it wasn't possible to talk intimately in such a cramped space. I had hopes for the walk along the shore, but, when we piled out of the buses on a sandy promontory about four miles along the coast from Weerdwood, the notion that we'd have a leisurely ramble was quickly scotched. Rusty divided us into two groups and, although Grace was in mine, strict supervision was on the menu once again.

"Single file, please, and no fooling about," said Rusty, who was to be our leader. "The path isn't dangerous but it's crumbly at the edge and I don't want anyone falling over."

As we hit the track that followed the shoreline high above the rocks, Grace smiled at me ruefully.

"Later," she said.

Tramping along and sniffing the salty air, I decided I might as well try to enjoy myself. My spirits always rose when I was away from Weerdwood, and I liked the way the estuary shone like a broken mirror in the sun. The scarves of sand and silver shingle uncovered by the ebb-tide were beautiful and there was an amazing view of mountains far away. Unexpectedly, I also found myself liking Rusty. We'd hardly have walked ten metres before he called our attention to something interesting – a clump of creamy primroses a breath away from opening, a cache of opalescent shells, a rabbit peeping from its burrow in the turf above. He pointed out birds, rock pipits and oystercatchers and red-throated divers, and told us how, if you were lucky, you could see seals and dolphins beyond Sutor Point. He was bursting with information.

"That's Ben Wyvis in the distance. I've seen snow up there in July. The ruined church in the gully is called Kilcurdie, 'the cell of Curitan'. He's one of our local saints. The village down there is Graceville. Admiral Weare built it for his estate workers and named it after his wife, Lady Grace Murray."

"Well, fancy," whispered Grace, giving me a wink, but by that time Rusty was on to something else.

You could tell the guy loved the place. His eyes sparkled and all his twitchiness melted away as he shared it with us. I thought it was a pity he had to waste so much time organising builders and sorting out business matters instead of teaching kids full time. I've never forgotten his large hands cradling a cream and brown striped snail-shell, or the careful way he put it back on the grass when he'd shown it to us. It wasn't until we were sitting on the rocks above the beach near Weerdwood, waiting for Jess and her group to catch us up, that I again sensed tension in him – and knew that he wasn't strictly telling the truth.

The tide had drawn the river right back, exposing a vast, wet shore. Among the pale shingle there was an area, perhaps a hundred metres wide, that was like sealskin lightly brushed with silver. Although gulls hopped everywhere else, they seemed to shun it. I saw that it was marked round its perimeter by wooden poles with red pennants fluttering in the breeze.

"What is that place, Rusty?" Grace asked suddenly. "Why the flags?"

He answered this openly.

"It's called Gabriel's Flow," he said. "It's a quicksand, and the flags are to warn people not to step on it."

"Is it dangerous then, sir?" asked Willie, who wasn't the world's brightest.

Rusty nodded.

"The minute you set foot on it, it would start to suck you down," he explained. "Unless there was someone on shore to raise the alarm at once, you'd be gripped and swallowed, like a snake digesting its prey. That's if you weren't drowned first."

"Drowned?" repeated Willie, saucer-eyed. "How so?"

"The tide here is freaky," Rusty said. "It flows at a terrifying speed – something to do with the pull of the quicksand and the instability of the gravel underwater. If you were already trapped and the tide was coming in, you'd be drowned long before the quicksand closed over you."

Gillian said, "Eek!" and gave one of her exaggerated shivers.

No one paid her attention, least of all me. Suddenly I had remembered Jake telling me in the garden that when Weerdwood first opened as a youth centre, a girl had drowned "in the quicksand down at Sutor Point". Glancing at Rusty's grim face, I wondered if he was thinking about her too. Grace went on staring at the dark stretch of sand.

"Has anyone stepped on it?" she inquired.

I could see a gleam of irritation in Rusty's eyes, but he answered calmly.

"A woman lost her dog a couple years back, I believe. She was a holidaymaker and didn't know to keep him on the lead. And there was a nasty incident once with some sheep that strayed from Weerdwood Mains."

True, probably, but not the whole truth.

"Who was Gabriel?" asked Grace sharply.

Rusty's patience had run out.

"Haven't a clue," he snapped.

Which might have been true, of course. Yet it seemed strange that a man so well acquainted with the land where he lived, who knew the names of places and how they'd got them, had a blank in his mind about this one. He was certainly relieved when Mary's voice called, "*Yoo hoo! Come on down!*" and we saw her, Jake and Cameron laden with barbecue and baskets, staggering down the slope from Weerdwood to the beach.

12

The Woman in White

The picnic lunch was the sort of occasion I'd imagined enjoying at Weerdwood, before the whole experience was ruined by supernatural events. While the walkers flopped about in the mild sunshine, Jake got the barbecue going and Mary unpacked the baskets. Soon a delicious smell of chargrilled sausages and chicken kebabs was floating along the beach. There was pitta bread stuffed with roasted vegetables, followed by baked bananas smothered in chocolate sauce. Mary was an amazing cook and we were all starving after our morning in the fresh air. Afterwards Rusty produced a ball and the boys started a kick-about on the sand. Most of the girls began to walk along the tideline, gathering shells and coloured pebbles to take home. As the adults cleared up the picnic debris, Grace and I climbed over the rocks, settling ourselves beside a bleached wooden post to which was hooked a red and white lifebelt and a coil of strong rope.

"Not much use to a sheep," said Grace. I was saved from having to respond by the arrival of Jake. He sat down on the sandy grass, stretching out his lanky legs and rubbing his back against the post. "Are you free?" asked Grace, in her mildly ironic way.

"I have a study afternoon," Jake told her. "I should be swotting for my biology exam, but I've got something else on my mind."

This was the first time I'd seen Grace and Jake together since he'd spilled the beans to her about his past. I watched them covertly, looking for any little sign that something might be taking off between them. Although the discovery that Jake had told Grace the truth about himself cleared me of any responsibility, I still thought a relationship between a posh girl like her and a streetwise tough like him was a disaster waiting to happen. I didn't sense any particular vibes between them just then, but I remained suspicious. They might be playing it cool on account of me, or it might just be that for the moment they were concentrating on other things.

Grace had scooped up a palmful of sand and was letting it trickle slowly through her fingers.

"What's on your mind?" she asked.

"I saw another ghost last night," Jake replied.

My eyes widened and I had to repress a little scream. I don't know why I should have been so taken aback, since Grace certainly wasn't. She leaned towards Jake and gave him a penetrating look.

"Tell me about it," she said.

Jake fiddled with his ear-studs.

"I'd done a late shift," he said, "helping Mary to chop the veg and get stuff out of the freezer for today. Then we had a cup of tea. I went upstairs about half eleven – my room's in the attic overlooking the garden. The heating at Weerdwood's very efficient and I've never once felt cold in the house. So it was a shock – about two-thirds of the way up the attic stair – to feel I was stepping into the Arctic. I thought my lungs would burst and, when I put my hand on the banister, it was like touching the element in a freezer. That was when I saw her, standing on the top step looking down at me."

Suddenly Jake's pale eyes blinked rapidly, and he had to bite his lip to keep it from trembling. Grace put out her hand and touched his arm.

"Just tell it like it was," she encouraged him.

Jake took a deep breath.

"She was about my age," he said. "She was wearing a long white dress embroidered with flowers, and a shawl hanging down from her arms. She had a lot of fair hair and – and – oh, strewth!" His face flooded with embarrassment. "How can I tell you this?"

Grace said it for him.

"She looked like me."

I've never seen anyone look simultaneously so shocked and so relieved.

"You know," Jake said.

Grace nodded.

"I saw her coming out of the sealed room yesterday

morning," she told him. "So like me, I thought I was seeing myself. I only saw her for a moment, then she disappeared."

"Did she disappear last night, Jake?" I asked.

He glanced at me as if he'd forgotten I was there.

"Not exactly," he replied. "She was only at the top of the stair for a moment, then she sort of faded away along the corridor and it was warm again. But later on, when I'd put out my light and drawn back the curtains, my eye was caught by a movement down below. The clouds were breaking up and the moon had rubbed through, so I could see quite clearly. The ghost was flitting up and down the path to the shrubbery – five, maybe six times, before she vanished again behind the bushes. She seemed all of a jitter – as if she was looking for something she couldn't find."

Even when you're scared rigid, you can still resent being ignored. So, when I saw Grace and Jake exchanging puzzled looks, I felt quite smug.

"She was looking for her dog," I said.

Two pairs of eyes switched their gaze to me. Jake's were questioning but Grace's were reproachful.

"Con!" she exclaimed. "You've seen her too. You might have told me last night."

She looked really upset and I hurried to explain.

"I wanted to tell you," I said, "but before I could Mrs Finch arrived and sent you to bed. Anyway, I haven't seen the ghost the way you two have. Before I came to Weerdwood, I kept having dreams about the house as it must have been long ago. In one of them I saw a portrait of the woman in white who looked like you, Grace. It was above the fireplace in the drawing-room, and it really was there because you can still see where it was hooked up. I noticed the resemblance when I met you, but I didn't mention it because – well, before you saw the dog for yourself you wouldn't have believed me. And once I knew that you were related to the Weares, it seemed less odd, because faces do recur in families."

I was interrupted by a splutter from Jake. Evidently, when he'd confided in Grace about his past, she hadn't returned the compliment. Now he stared at her as if she was a rare monkey at the zoo.

"Related to the Weares?" he repeated incredulously. "As in Admiral the Earl of? Well, pardon me, your ladyship."

"Shut your face," said Grace crisply. "Go on about the portrait, Con."

"The young woman was standing against a background of trees," I said, "wearing the dress Jake just described. She had a dog beside her – a deerhound, the spit of the one we keep seeing now."

Jake clicked his tongue and Grace covered her face with her hands.

"Oh, my God," she groaned.

We sat in silence for a while, watching our companions enjoying a normal day on a normal school trip. The same questions repeated themselves in my head. "Why us? Why me?" A haze had veiled the morning sun and suddenly it was bitterly cold. Grace got up, shivering as she reached for her purple fleece.

"Jake," she said. "That quicksand called Gabriel's Flow. Have you any idea who Gabriel was?"

I felt slightly impatient that she was still harping on about this, as if we didn't have really flaky things to worry us. Jake pushed himself onto his feet and brushed the sand off his jeans.

"I didn't even know that was its name," he said. "I don't know anything about this area and to be honest, I don't like it. There's something about the way the water shivers and the mist creeps – it'd be spooky, even without the spooks."

He walked away abruptly on the sandy track towards Weerdwood, just as Mrs Finch drove up in the minibus and Rusty blew a whistle to summon the stragglers on the beach.

All the QM girls were excellent swimmers, but Grace was the best. Her strokes were strong and elegant, her diving almost flawless. I could get my feet off the bottom, but my style was more frog than mermaid. On our previous visits to Poyntz Community Centre, Grace had swum with me and given me some coaching, showing me how to push out with my legs and breathe regularly, instead of splashing and panting like a nervous puppy. Today, however, she left me to footle about at the shallow end while she swam endless lengths of the pool, cutting through the water with her gleaming arms and legs. I didn't mind, because I knew she needed time to consider – and so did I. We were back in the bus before I ventured to say quietly, "Grace, I was thinking. Perhaps if we knew who the woman in white was, it might help us to understand what all this is about. I wondered – if maybe you could ask your mum."

It was only then that I realised how deeply hurt Grace had been by the letter her mother had sent her. Her brows

84

contracted and the unforgiving compression of her lips hardened her jaw and made her look much older.

"After what she said to me, I shan't ask her anything," she said coldly. "The way I feel now, I don't ever want to speak to her again."

There was no suitable reply. As Mrs Finch drove us back along the now familiar coast road, I sat with my embarrassed face turned to the window. The tide was racing in, swirling like cream wool over the damp sand. Gabriel's Flow was already covered, with only the tops of the flagpoles marking where it lay. It occurred to me suddenly that I hadn't seen or heard the phantom deerhound for more than twenty-four hours. Had it been reunited with the woman in white, I wondered and, if so, would that be an end of the haunting? Wishful thinking – from which I was diverted by Grace's hand on my sleeve.

"Con, I'm sorry," she whispered. "I shouldn't have snapped at you. Of course it would be interesting to know who the ghost was. It's just that I can't ask Mum and just now I can't think of anyone else. Thanks for the thought, anyway."

I thought this response was a bit feeble, but I realised it was all I'd get for now.

As Mrs Finch braked in the courtyard behind the Underwood Academy bus and we all climbed out, the builders were getting ready to leave. It wasn't hard to imagine what was heaped under the tarpaulin in the back of their truck, and there was other evidence that they'd had a busy day. Beside the front steps lay a pile of bricks, broken and dabbled with black paint. Above the door, a new window had been fitted and the sill re-plastered. In the entrance hall, we looked up through a large square hole in the ceiling, cut from the floor of the mysterious room.

After he'd spoken to the foreman, Rusty's relief was palpable.

"No dry rot and the lift will be in by the end of April," he said, grinning with satisfaction.

Most people had drifted off down the passage to Admiral's Lodge when Grace started raking through her pockets.

"Damn, I must dropped my watch in the minibus," she said. "Mrs Finch, may I have the keys?"

"You'll lose your head next," said Mrs Finch resignedly as she opened her bag.

I went out with Grace, stamping my feet on the frosty paving while she unlocked the door and scrabbled about on the floor of the bus.

"OK. Got it," she said. "I must remember to get the strap mended on Saturday."

When we came back indoors, one weak overhead bulb was switched on in the hall. By its dismal light we saw the deerhound, sitting disconsolately on the landing halfway up the dusty stair. He raised his grey head hopefully as we entered, then uttered a puppy's yelp of disappointment and loss. Tears pricked my eyes as he came slinking downstairs with drooping tail, edged past us and disappeared into the wintry dusk.

"So she hasn't found him," Grace said.

13

Absent Without Leave

"Stop that, you mean cow!"

"Give it back!"

"It's *mine*!"

"*Liar*! You're always nicking my stuff. Why don't you buy your own bloody body spray?"

There was a colossal thump, then wailing like a banshee in pain.

"Help! Stop! Ow-www!"

Eyes sparkling with delight, Gillian opened our bedroom door and we all tumbled out into the passage. Other doors were opening and avid faces popping out. I could feel my jaw dropping with disbelief. Grace in a pink and white nightie and Isabelle in a blue fleece dressing-gown (even at QM they didn't have to wear uniform in bed) were sprawling on the floor outside the shower rooms, going at each other like two wildcats. Grace had Isabelle in an armlock and the fingers of her left hand were embedded in Isabelle's thick red hair. Isabelle drummed her heels and howled for assistance.

"Help! Mrs Finch! Grace Kendrick's trying to kill me!"

Mrs Finch came out of Room 7 like a bull in a plaid dressing-gown. Thundering past us down the passage, she stood over the wrestling pair, her grey hair on end and her red cheeks quivering with indignation.

"Stop it at once!" she bellowed. "Get up, both of you, *now!*" Grace and Isabelle parted reluctantly and scrambled to their feet. Isabelle was whimpering and Grace was panting, her face fixed in a mutinous scowl. Mrs Finch glared at them, her eyes popping with anger and incredulity. "I have never," she said, "been so ashamed in my life. See me in the games room after breakfast and prepare to be very afraid."

Unfortunately, before we could see how the two fighters would react, Miss Gallacher, also in her dressing-gown, arrived on the scene.

"Back to your rooms, please," she said briskly to the spectators from Underwood Academy. "This has nothing to do with you."

Which was true of the others, but not entirely of me. I could think of several occasions during the past few days when Grace, who had initially seemed such a calm, good-natured girl, had either lost her cool with me completely or seemed on the brink of doing so. She'd been disarmingly apologetic afterwards, and I'd put it down to her being under stress because of seeing ghosts – particularly one who was her double. But this tantrum was in another league and, as I closed our bedroom door, I wondered for the first time whether there might be an even more arcane explanation. The thought filled me with apprehension, but I was still far from understanding what the problem might be.

I don't know what Mrs Finch said to Grace and Isabelle in the games room, but, when they came out late to the garden, Grace looked the more upset of the two. Taking a hoe from Jess she went off to weed gravel along the edges of the main path, while Isabelle was sent to sow seeds in the potting shed. I was scraping moss off the ornamental balustrades on either side of the steps, and watching the deerhound pursuing his endless quest among the trees. I still hadn't seen the woman in white outside her picture frame, but I couldn't help wondering whether it was her unseen presence that made the shadows in the garden darker and fed my dread that terrible happenings lay ahead.

At morning break, Grace came to sit beside me in the dining-room. It was so cold outside that we were glad to shelter there. I'd thought she might be too ashamed to mention the morning's brawl, but she was perfectly open about it.

"Never let your parents send you to boarding-school, Con. Being banged up with stupid women makes you do stupid things. I bet it's the same in the nick."

I had a snowball in hell's chance of being sent to boarding-school and the sour thought occurred to me that Jake would be more clued up about the nick. All I said was, "Have you made up?"

"With Isabelle? Don't make me laugh. I don't like being

in Finchy's bad books, though. She invites me to stay in the holidays and she's a star."

Which made what happened later in the day even more mysterious. In the afternoon, Grace disappeared. Because we were spread out all over the garden, it wasn't until knocking-off time at four o'clock that anyone noticed she was missing. I'd been cold and preoccupied; it was only when we returned our tools to the potting shed and Jess asked, "Where's Grace?" that I realised I hadn't seen her since lunch. Apparently no one else had either, but Jess wasn't immediately alarmed.

"Go and find her, Con," she said, with a trace of annoyance. "I want to get the shed locked up and get into a hot shower. Push off, the rest of you. I'll wait."

There was a stillness in the garden like the hush that precedes snow. Even the rooks and gulls were silent and the motionless branches were like a net drawn with charcoal against the heavy, yellowish sky. Scared of the ghosts yet desperate to find Grace, I scurried along the path to the place where she'd been weeding earlier in the day. There was no sign of her, only her hoe leaning against the wall. Alarm rose to terror as I doubled back along the edge of the trees, calling, "Grace! Grace, are you there?" My voice was swallowed by the shadows of the wood.

Everyone else had gone indoors. There were lights in the windows of Admiral's Lodge and I could hear a radio blasting out music, but the rest of the house brooded darkly, its empty belfry and broken chimneys spiking the sky. By now I was in such a panic that I hardly knew where I was going.

Crashing round the minibuses in the courtyard, I began to run down the drive. "Grace, Grace, where are you?" I was almost at the gate when I noticed the gleam of gold in the short grass of the verge. It was Grace's watch – the one she kept in her pocket because the catch on the wrist-band had broken. It caught on her handkerchief and several times she'd nearly lost it. *Almost at the gate.* I snatched the watch up and pelted back to the potting shed, where Jess was trotting to and fro trying to keep warm. If she was furious, her mood changed as she saw my terrified face.

"I found it – grass – end of the drive," I gasped, waving the watch in front of Jess. "I think – Grace has done a runner."

I only saw Jess's horrified look for an instant before her booted feet thundered away through the darkening garden. By the time I'd got my breath back and made it to the front door, every adult in the house, including Jake, was in the courtyard. Rusty was barking orders.

"Jess, get your bike and go towards Poyntz. Mary, comb the grounds – the kid may have come back and be hiding somewhere. Jake, go with Mrs Finch and search along the shore. I'll take my car up the Cromar Road."

"What about me?" asked Miss Gallacher.

"You'll stay here and mind the other kids," said Rusty. He glanced at his watch, then added tersely, "Call me on your mobile if you find her. If I haven't heard by five-fifteen, I'll ring the police."

As they scattered, I got a glimpse of their taut, shocked faces. This was teachers' worst nightmare come true.

I hid in the empty games room because I couldn't bear to

share the excitement upstairs. There's a horrible atmosphere in a group of kids when there's an accident or someone goes missing, anxiety spiced with morbid speculation and a relish for gory details that can easily tip over into hysteria. I didn't want to hear myself screaming, "Shut up, Gillian, who cares what you think about anything?" I didn't put the light on, but left the door open a crack so that I could see into the hall. Among the shadowy pool tables and exercise machines, I grieved for Grace as if she was already dead.

I don't how many tense minutes had passed before I heard the front door opening and peeped out into the hall. When I saw Grace entering between Jake and Mrs Finch, I was ready to burst out and throw myself into her arms – only to be stopped by the eruption of energy behind them as Rusty catapulted into the hall.

I know that adults are always at their angriest when a kid has scared the pants off them; Mum only ever thumped me once, when I'd fallen in Dunkley's pond after she'd told me repeatedly not to go there. Even so, Rusty's reaction was way over the top. His face was purple and his beard twitching, and he kept clenching and unclenching his fists as if he was having trouble keeping his hands off Grace.

"You stupid little fool," he hollered. "Have you any idea the trouble you've caused? How often do you have to be told to obey rules made for your own safety? What've you got to say for yourself, eh?"

"That will do, Mr Cooper!"

Clearly angered, Mrs Finch put a protective arm round Grace's shoulders. But Grace stood like a statue, her face impassive and her eyes peculiarly bright. Moving away from Mrs Finch, she looked disdainfully at Rusty.

"I was looking for my dog," she said.

Mrs Finch came late to supper and Grace didn't appear at all. Afterwards Mrs Finch, taking pity on my anxious face, drew me aside in the hall.

"Try not to worry," she said, which was rich coming from someone as obviously bothered as she was. "I don't know how much Grace has told you about herself, but when she was a little girl she saw her dog run down and killed on the road. One way and another she had a difficult childhood, and I'm afraid this visit to the place where her ancestors lived has been more traumatic than enjoyable. I've given her something to help her sleep and I'll take her to the doctor in Poyntz in the morning, just to be on the safe side."

On the safe side! You wonder about adults sometimes. Just for a moment, I was tempted to pour out the truth, to tell Mrs Finch that Grace and Jake and I were spooked out of our heads and that Weerdwood was the least safe place on earth, with its apparitions and its tragic, short-lived family and its choking sense of doom. It wasn't fear of Rusty or even of angering Jake that stopped me. It was the sad awareness that no grown-up – not even kind Mrs Finch – would believe my story was anything but the imagining of a silly, impressionable kid. There would be two of us going to the doctor in Poyntz in the morning, 'to be on the safe side'.

I sat through the evening's entertainment, a talk and slide-show on the wildlife of the Highlands, of which I took in absolutely nothing. When it was over, there was hot chocolate and cookies in the dining-room, dispensed by Jake. I didn't know whether to have any, but finally decided that a mug of chocolate might help me to sleep. That was why I was last in the queue, and Jake was able to speak to me without being overheard.

"Make an excuse and come into the kitchen," he said. "I'm on duty alone and I need a word with you."

"What about?" I asked suspiciously.

"Just come," he replied.

I wasn't keen to be alone with him, but I was wildly curious to know where Grace had been found and what he wanted to talk to me about. Reckoning quickly that the dining-room was full of people and that if I hollered in the kitchen someone would be bound to hear me, I said, "Well, OK."

It was the first time in my life I'd ever knocked over a mug deliberately. The hot chocolate spread stickily, some of it splashing the tablecloth, but most of it landing on the polished wooden floor.

"Oh, hell! Go and ask Jake for a cloth," said Jess irritably.

None of our adults was in a sweet mood that evening.

"Right," I said.

I don't know what I expected Jake to say and, if I was surprised, it was only because he seemed so gobsmacked. As I came through the swing-door, he was loading the dishwasher. He turned to face me with a dirty plate in his hands. His face was ashen.

"Con," he said, coming straight to the point. "That posh girl, Grace. You don't think she fancies me, do you?"

Even in the most terrible situations, you sometimes want to laugh.

"What makes you think that?" I inquired, trying to repress a smirk.

"When I found her this afternoon," said Jake, "sitting on the rocks down at Sutor Point as if she'd every right to be there, she – er, sort of came on –" His cheeks went suddenly pink with embarrassment. "I thought she was making a pass at me," he muttered.

"She thinks you look like David Beckham," I told him.

I don't know whether he was more amazed or appalled.

"You're joking. No? Aw, *Jesus*," he groaned.

14

Old Clothes

That night not even a whole pack of baying hounds would have kept me awake. I was so pooped after my interview with Jake that I could hardly stagger upstairs. I went to the loo, but didn't even bother cleaning my teeth. While Gillian and Anne were still chewing over Grace's escapade, I crawled into bed, pulled up my duvet and went out like a light. I had a fantastic night's sleep and I needed it, since the next day things were to become even more alarming and weird.

Despite the leaden sky and piercing cold of Thursday afternoon, it had only snowed on Ben Wyvis, the mountain that rose like a vast iced birthday cake on the other side of the firth. Down at sea level we had wind-driven sleet, melting as it touched the ground and once more filling the garden with mini-bogs and pools. It was plain, on Friday morning, that we were going to spend another day working indoors. *Never mind*, I tried to console myself as I got dressed. *One week from today, I'll be on my way home*. Only by then Weerdwood had become a little world where ordinary time was strangely meaningless.

"If you all work hard, we'll finish painting the bedrooms today," said Rusty.

He was doing his best to be upbeat, I dare say, but he looked absolutely drained, his cheeks a greyish colour and his eyes dull with lost sleep. If he hadn't been so foul to Grace, I'd really have felt sorry for him. Grace and Mrs Finch hadn't appeared at breakfast and I'd assumed Grace was still in bed. I was surprised, as we gathered in the hall to put on our overalls, to see them come in from the courtyard, back from an early appointment at Poyntz Health Centre.

"How did you get on?" I asked Grace, when she joined me shortly afterwards among the ladders and pots of paint.

"It was a fuss about nothing," she replied tartly. "Since when has it been a sign of mental disturbance to get fed up weeding and go for a walk on the shore? That's what I told the doctor, and he said he didn't blame me. Oh, and his name's Dr Carberry, by the way."

"Did he give you a prescription?" I wanted to know.

"He gave Finchy a flea in her ear," replied Grace, with a heartless giggle. She glooped some yellow paint from a tin into a tray and ran a roller through it. "Well, back to hard labour. I blame the Duke of Edinburgh for all of this," she sighed.

No one in the orange group was in a talkative mood that

morning. Even Cameron and Willie seemed subdued, perhaps by the darkness that shrouded the house and made the interior even more oppressive. We had the light on, one harsh overhead bulb that threw thin, distorted shadows across the bare walls. I didn't mind a bit of quiet, because I had plenty to think about.

When we'd come upstairs, I'd had goosebumps at the prospect of seeing again the strange room above the front door. When I did, however, its mystery was gone. The door had been taken off its hinges and the light from the new window revealed walls largely stripped of their scabby, faintly rose-patterned wallpaper. The whole floor had been taken up to cut the gaping hole we could see from the hall downstairs, where brick walls were already going up to make the shell of the wheelchair lift-shaft. Across the doorway there was fluorescent tape and a big notice saying DANGER KEEP OUT – just in case anyone was daft enough to walk into a room with no floor. In the corridor I noticed a dusty walnut wardrobe which hadn't been there previously, but even that didn't disturb me. Yet as I painted the room where, in the summer, children would sleep, I couldn't help reliving the terrible morning when a ghost – seen differently by three people and not at all by many more – had escaped into the world of the living.

That it was Grace's ancestor wasn't in doubt, although we still had no idea who the young woman in the portrait was. Indeed, to be completely truthful, we didn't know whether the portrait had ever existed outside my dream. The hooks on the drawing-room wall might have supported another painting altogether, although I didn't think so. The peacock wallpaper of my dream was still there, after all, and the windows and chandelier were just as I'd seen them in my bed at home. The ghost hadn't been seen again after Jake had watched her disappear among the trees, although the phantom deerhound was never far away. Grace and I saw and heard him so often that we'd become almost blasé, but it was clear that he scared the pants off Jake. No doubt his close encounters with the dog and the savaging of his denim jacket had added to his sense of insecurity. Why the animal should dislike Jake particularly was just one mystery among many.

And then, there was Grace. As I watched her rolling paint onto the wall beside the window, I couldn't help thinking that Dr Carberry – no relation of mine – hadn't been very perceptive. Grace looked ghastly, panda-eyed and obviously on edge; once or twice when Miss Gallacher, who was supervising our group, said quite pleasantly, "Look, Grace, you've missed a bit there," Grace had glowered and flounced and practically thrown the paint against the wall. To be fair to Dr Carberry, he had probably been pushed for time and Grace wasn't his patient. Besides, she'd have spoken to him with the self-confidence that made all the QM girls seem more grown up than they really were. And he couldn't have known how speedily Grace had changed from a friendly, well-mannered person into an intermittently bad-tempered and haughty one – though not too haughty to throw herself at a Paisley tough who, thank God, didn't seem smitten in return.

"I've got a girlfriend in Glasgow," Jake had told me in the kitchen. "Her mum was my buddy – that's a prison visitor who takes an interest in you. Her name's Carly and we really like each other. She's got a place at Liverpool University, and I'm going to apply there if I get the grades I need in the summer. The last thing I need is a posh kid taking a fancy to me because she thinks I look like some poncy footballer."

I had refused his request to tell Grace to back off, thinking it was none of my business, but I was relieved to have one less thing to worry about.

I suppose what shocked me most was that even Mrs Finch, whom Grace loved, had now been the object of a cruel remark. I felt really sorry for Mrs Finch, who was the nicest teacher I'd ever known. She knew there was something the matter, but, being an adult, made the wrong connections. She thought that Grace's strange statement, "I was looking for my dog," was linked to the trauma of losing a childhood pet. I reckoned the dog Grace was talking about was a whole lot closer to her right now and, although I didn't yet understand what was happening, alarm bells weren't half ringing in my head.

It was my experience at Weerdwood that, although on one level everything was entirely predictable, on another surprise followed horrible surprise. As usual, we had a coffee break at eleven and, as we came back through the drawing-room, I saw Grace examining the peacock wallpaper with a pensive expression on her face.

"I've seen this paper before," she told me. "It's a William

Morris design. Con, when you dreamt this room, do you remember the carpet?"

"Not really," I said.

"It was Persian," Grace said positively. "It had a dark blue background with rectangles and diamonds of gold and green." I think she'd have said more, but, catching my startled eye, she backtracked hurriedly. "I mean – well, that's what would've suited the wallpaper best, don't you think?"

Before I could reply, she walked away from me abruptly through the door to the landing. When I followed I found a scene so amazing that it put everything else right out of my head.

Coming upstairs first thing, I'd noticed the wardrobe in the passage, its curved doors secured by two tarnished brass handles. It had crossed my mind that it must have come from the haunted room, but, my mind full of other things, I hadn't paid it any attention. While we had been having our snack, Rusty had decided to open it, and the suffocating smell of damp, rotting fabric filled the landing where he was laying out the contents on the floor.

"Hey, come and look at this, kids," he said, no doubt still pursuing his policy of 'openness'. Some people never learn.

It's painful to recall the horror and pity I felt as I gazed at the pathetic relics of a dead girl's life; a straw hat scabbed with green mould, a moth-eaten fur cloak, disintegrating leather bags and cracked patent shoes. There were damp scarves and underwear in filthy cardboard boxes, wormy things that were probably stockings, soiled dresses that had once been beautiful silk and velvet – a lady's fine possessions ruined by the careless but implacable passing of time. The boys barely looked before drifting back to their painting. The girls gathered round, exclaiming sorrowfully over the wreck of so much desirable gear.

"What a shame! Look at these shoes. They would've been to die for when they were new."

"A pity about the dresses. The material's all gone to holes. You couldn't possibly mend them."

"Have you no idea who they belonged to, Rusty?"

Rusty shook his head.

"Some Lady Weare, I suppose," he said.

I was jerked out of my own sad contemplation by Grace's hand tugging sharply at my sleeve. She didn't look distressed, only puzzled and slightly put out.

"Con! Where's the white dress – the one with the roses?" she asked sharply.

"You said that when she came out of the sealed room she was wearing it," I heard myself reply.

"Oh, yes, of course. So I was," Grace said.

15

A Chill in the Night

Jake had been right when he said that the heating at Weerdwood was very efficient. Indeed it was sometimes too efficient, even for someone like me who preferred to be cosy. Quite often I'd had to shed layers of clothing indoors and at night, even with the window open a fraction and the curtains pulled back, our bedroom could be quite stuffy. It had been as warm as usual when Miss Gallacher put out the light and once again I'd flaked out almost at once. After another perplexed and anxious day, there was nothing I'd have welcomed more than nine hours of unbroken sleep. So I was both surprised and annoyed when I woke in the dark and realised why. My bed was so cold that the sheet and duvet felt damp and the pillow, when I shifted my cheek, was like a lump of ice. Raising my head, I peered at the fluorescent numbers on my bedside clock: 02:05.

Oh, hell, I thought. *The central heating's gone phut and it's still five hours till getting up time*.

I lay for a while with the duvet humped over me, drawing up my freezing feet inside my pyjama trousers and blowing on my hands to try and warm them. There wasn't a sound to be heard: no howling dog, no breath of wind in the trees, no faint hum of traffic on the motorway beyond the fields. I needed to widdle. Reluctance to get up fought with reluctance to wet myself – no contest, when your bladder is about to burst. Crawling out of bed, I groped for my slippers on carpet that felt like frosted grass. As I put on my dressing-gown I was shaking and my teeth were chattering like castanets.

There was a faint ribbon of light under the door; a lamp was always left on in the passage so that you didn't have to blunder to the loo in the dark. As I gently turned the handle, I glimpsed Anne and Gillian fast asleep, Gillian with both arms and one leg protruding from the duvet. It went though my mind that she'd get frostbite. The passage was even colder than the bedroom, if that was possible. As I padded along to the toilet-room I could see my breath vaporising in front of me and my chest was tight with pain.

Then I saw her. She was floating down the narrow corridor, an icy spectre dressed entirely in white. Her face and bare arms were as pale as marble, her hair like the angel-snow people use to decorate their Christmas trees. Only her eyes were gas-flame blue, burning intensely as they stared into mine. As she drifted towards me over the green carpet I was frozen, and not just with cold. Sheer terror paralysed me. I couldn't go back, or even move to the wall to avoid her.

Please God, don't let her touch me, I prayed. My prayer was answered, in the strangest possible way.

The ghost was a couple of metres from me when she began to change, as if her body had been stroked by a warm hand. Colour suffused her hair, turning white to gold. The ghastly pallor of her face was touched by normal colour. The roses on her dress faded, leaving the fabric plain. Grace stood barefoot in her nightie outside the toilet room door, her hair tousled and her eyes screwed up against the light.

"Oh, it's you, Con," she said. "I need a wee and a drink of water. I can't sleep for the heat in this place. It was never like this in the old days."

It was true that the atmosphere had changed, as if Arctic cold had been blasted by African sun. As I sat on the toilet, I heard Grace tinkling in the next cubicle, the soft flush of the loo and the glug of the bottled water dispenser as she filled a paper cup. She left without speaking, which was just as well, since I wasn't fit to make a coherent reply.

My close encounter with the ghost had been absolutely terrifying, but so was the realisation of what it meant. Back in my perfectly warm and comfortable bed, I remembered that when I had perceived a shadowy figure and Jake had seen 'something abnormal' issuing from the walled-up room, Grace had seen herself. So wasn't that what the ghost had seen too, someone so like herself that she didn't know the difference? She had invaded Grace's space, making her think thoughts that weren't hers. She was gradually replacing Grace's personality with her own, injecting into her memory things she couldn't possibly have known – like the pattern on the drawing-room carpet and the temperature in the house long ago.

"Con! Where's the white dress – the one with the roses?"

"You said that when she came out of the sealed room she was wearing it."

"Oh, yes, of course, so I was."

The worst thing was not knowing where to turn for help. For what adult, I thought despairingly, would take seriously anything so mind-bogglingly weird? Not Rusty, not Mrs Finch, not the shrink on whose couch I'd be lying if this nightmare went on for much longer. Perhaps most chillingly, I reckoned Grace wouldn't believe it either.

As the minibus bowled over the Kessock Bridge next morning, taking the girls on a Saturday shopping trip to Inverness, I sat watching Grace out of the corner of my eye. When the QM girls went out, they had to wear proper school uniform – violet wool trouser suits and pale mauve shirts. The gear suited some of them better than others, but I thought most of them looked like clones. Only Grace didn't look like anyone else; she was too beautiful, a swan among geese. She was staring out of the window at the choppy grey water of the Moray Firth, and I wondered nervously what was going on inside her head. She must have felt my eyes on her, for she turned and smiled at me. She looked so nice and normal that for a moment I thought perhaps my awful night thoughts been mistaken.

"What are you thinking about?" she asked half teasingly.

"That you look nice," I said. "The colour suits you."

Grace laughed and gave me a gentle push.

"I hate it," she said. "I look dire in strong colours. The nicest dress I have is the white one I wore when Rupert Molinar painted my portrait."

I felt myself stiffen. But unlike yesterday, when she'd backtracked on her remark about the carpet, Grace seemed quite unaware that she'd said anything strange. She turned back to the window, her forefinger idly doodling on the glass. As the minibus ran down the slip road and headed for the centre of Inverness, I held my tote bag close to my chest, trying to still my wildly beating heart.

As things turned out, I didn't see much more of Grace during the day. When we got out in the carpark, all the posh girls scampered off to use their American Express cards at Jigsaw and Karen Millen, with a resigned Mrs Finch in tow. The rest of us spent the morning trailing round Etam and Dorothy Perkins with Miss Gallacher, trying on skimpy summer clothes you couldn't imagine it ever being warm enough to wear. I bought a T-shirt for Mum and socks for Mark in Debenhams, and a pair of white ankle-boots for myself at Nine West. My pocket money exhausted, I window-shopped and worried about Grace.

At lunch-time we met up with the boys, who had been to a gym with Rusty. After a bite to eat, we went to the cinema to see *Harry Potter and the Chamber of Secrets*. Willie, who was next to me, thought it was cool, but I reckoned life at Hogwarts School was a breeze compared with life at Weerdwood. Back on the minibus, I wasn't able to bag a seat beside Grace, because Mrs Finch had already sat down beside her. It was Gillian who plonked herself down beside me, dumping her H&M carrier bag on my knee while she fastened her seat belt.

"Con," she said, giving me a close look, "are you all right, pet?"

Gillian's mum called everybody 'pet' and it was catching.

"Why?"

"You look ghastly," said Gillian candidly. "All white, as if you'd seen a ghost."

I let this pass.

"I'm all right," I said. "I haven't been sleeping very well."

"Ach, well, never mind," consoled Gillian. "We'll soon be home and it'll be the Easter holidays. I'm having a sleepover for my birthday – just you and my cousin Kimberley from Tranent. We'll go to the Blue Lagoon for our tea and Mum's getting us tickets for *Les Misérables* at the Playhouse."

I felt a sudden rush of affection for Gillian. OK, she was bossy and she never thought twice before she opened her mouth, but she was kind-hearted and she came from the same world as I did. Accepting one of her chocolate toffees, I experienced an overwhelming desire for my familiar, ordinary life.

"Oh, yes! Thanks, Gill. That'll be great," I said.

16

The Co-Walker

As I'd realised guiltily when I was buying their presents, I'd
hardly thought about Mum and Mark during the last week.
They'd sent me postcards from Portugal and a couple of e-
mails, so I knew they were OK, and it had passed through
my mind on Friday morning that they'd be home later that
day. But once I'd decided to stick it out at Weerdwood,
ghostly matters had absorbed me and I hadn't got round to
writing to them. Even my feeling of homesickness on the
minibus had faded by the time I'd sucked Gillian's toffee off
my teeth. It came as a surprise and also a slight embarrassment
when, during a table-tennis tournament in the games room on
Saturday evening, Miss Gallacher came in and beckoned
me with her finger.

"Your mum's just rung," she told me. "I told her you were
fine, but she wants to talk to you. You can take the call in
Rusty's office. I've left the phone off the hook."

"Oh, dear. Sorry," I said.

Miss Gallacher grinned. She wasn't my favourite teacher, but she could be nice sometimes.

"You've done well, Con," she said warmly. "I'm really proud of you. But sometimes mums miss their kids more than their kids miss them."

This certainly seemed true of mine. When I picked up the phone in Rusty's overcrowded, paper-strewn office, I could sense her pleasure at hearing my voice. There was also a strong undertone of complaint.

"Con! I was sure I'd find a note from you when I got home. Why haven't you written? I gave you stamps."

"Yeah, I know. I meant to, but we don't have much spare time here. I thought you'd know I was OK." Hearing a sniff, I hurried on. "I'm fine," I lied. "Did you have cool time in Portugal?"

"It was lovely. I brought you a nice present."

"Thanks. I've got something for you too."

There was a lot of burbling at Mum's end, something about how she'd bought a cookery book and was going to make a nice Portuguese-style meal to welcome me home, if she could get red mullet and fresh mussels at Tesco. I kept saying, "Yeah, cool," and "Sounds yummy," but I was on autopilot by then. I'd just noticed something that dried my mouth and made the hair prickle at the nape of my neck.

On the wall above Rusty's desk there was a picture in a plain wooden frame. It was a print, shrunk from a much larger painting and much paler, but it was as familiar to me as the posters in my bedroom at home. The young woman whose strange transformation into Grace Kendrick I'd witnessed in the passage last night, looked at me through the dusty glass. Her right hand rested on the bodice of her white dress and her left caressed the fine head of her huge grey dog. Peering nervously, I read what was printed on the discoloured cardboard mount.

LADY HARRIET WEARE 1913
by RUPERT MOLINAR RSA
reproduced by permission of The Weerdwood Trust

"Con!" Mum's voice was quite sharp. "Are you still there?"

"What? Yes, but – sorry, Mum. I've got to go now. It's table-tennis and I'm due to play."

Another lie – I'd been knocked out by Isabelle in the first round. I knew Mum would be offended, but the air was cold again and I could almost feel the ghost of Lady Harriet Weare nearby. Whimpering, I banged down the phone and pelted out of the office – slap into the arms of Jake Gillanders, who was walking through the hall from the kitchen.

"Steady, Con," he said in surprise.

I was too distraught to pull away from him. Leaning my face on his chest, I began to cry like a baby.

"I – I – picture, office," I sobbed.

My old enemy couldn't have been kinder. Drawing me into a little alcove outside the office, he made me sit down and sat beside me.

"OK," he said, pulling a wad of tissues out of his pocket and sticking one into my hand. "Tell Uncle Piggy all about it."

I couldn't help smiling. I wiped my eyes and blew my nose, then I let it all come pouring out: about the wallpaper and the carpet and the old clothes; about Grace's scary remark about wearing her white dress to sit for Rupert Molinar; about seeing the ghost and how it had turned into Grace.

"I've been so frightened and worried," I said. "Something awful is happening to Grace and I don't know what to do. I can't mention ghosts in case Rusty goes ballistic and blames you for spreading rumour, and in any case, who would believe me? Then when I went into the office to speak to my mum on the phone, I saw the picture – the one that was in my dream. It *was* painted by someone called Rupert Molinar. It was so spooky, Jake. I just couldn't take any more."

I'd felt a tension in Jake when I'd spoken of the ghost melting into Grace, but now he just looked puzzled.

"Is there a picture?" he asked.

"Above the desk," I replied.

"Hang on." Jake got up and sprinted into the office. In a moment he was back, goggling in amazement. "You're right," he said, as if I might have been wrong. "God knows how often I've been in there, but I've never even noticed there was a picture. So now the ghost has a name. I wonder if Grace would recognise it."

"I'd be scared to ask her," I said.

"Yeah." Jake nodded in agreement. "It would be risky, considering the bad shape she's in. I must say I've been puzzled by the change in her," he added. "At the beginning, she was the one pushing for answers, but now it's like she's on another planet half the time." He fingered his ear-studs

112

for a moment, then he went on: "When I first met her, I thought she was nice – not my type or my class, but not snobby like a lot of the Hooray Henriettas that fetch up here. Now, when she's not trying to flirt with me, she treats me like her footman. And the day she ran away, she was seriously strange."

"How so?"

Jake scratched his fair head.

"I think I mentioned she was sitting on the rocks," he said. "What I didn't tell you was that her eyes were, like, glazed and she was talking to herself."

"Could you hear what she said?"

"Sure. It was a rhyme," Jake said. "I haven't been able to get it out of my head since.

> *When Gabriel cries*
> *Over bank and on brae,*
> *The children of Weerdwood*
> *Shall all wede away.*

When I asked her what the hell she was blethering about, she got all hoity-toity and said she didn't know what I meant."

"So you think –"

"I haven't known what to think," said Jake soberly, "but after what you told me about the ghost fading into Grace –" He paused thoughtfully, then continued. "Last year I did a course in social studies, and there was a module on folklore and superstition. It was really interesting, about the things people believed before the scientific age. I read about a belief in a ghost that was common to most of the peoples of

Europe – in Germany they called it a *doppelgänger* and in Britain a 'co-walker'."

You had to hand it to him. The guy had located his brains and learned to use them.

"And?" I prompted.

"Your co-walker was your ghostly double," Jake told me. "It was always with you, your evil counterpart, constantly trying to influence your thoughts and turn you into the opposite of your true self."

A sudden shiver raised gooseflesh on my arms.

"I thought of something like that in bed last night," I said. "It's the only explanation for the way Grace is behaving and the things she's saying. The ghost of Lady Harriet has seen her and wants to possess her."

Jake nodded, a frown wrinkling his white forehead. He ran his hand over his jaw, then he said tightly, "There's another superstition about co-walkers. To see your own was a warning of your death. I thought it was way-out when I first read it, but, after what I've been through here, I've a lot more respect for unscientific ideas."

"Does that mean – you think Grace is going to die?"

I could scarcely believe I was uttering these dreadful words.

Jake didn't answer directly.

"I believe she's in great danger," he said, "from the spirit of someone whose name we now know, but about whom we know nothing else. I also think you and I are the only ones who have any chance of protecting her, because – for some obscure reason – we're haunted too and can understand the danger she's in. And we might do that better if we knew something about the person we're up against, other than that she had a bloody great deerhound who's taken against me."

It was hard even to glimpse, in this clear-sighted, brave young man, the repulsive little bully of Barony Crescent. I was pleased that I was able immediately to contribute an idea.

"Come to church," I said.

"Eh?"

"Tomorrow, come to church. I went last week and the place is full of memorials to the Weares. There's a lot of information on them and they mostly tell you how the people died."

Jake looked leery.

"I haven't been to church since I was a pageboy at my Aunt Ag's wedding," he objected, "and then my mum skelped me for peeing on the carpet."

"You won't get skelped if you don't pee," I said impatiently, then wondered how I'd dared.

"OK." Jake made up his mind. "I have a couple of days off, actually. I have to go to Inverness on Monday, but I suppose tomorrow I can crawl out of my sack before lunch-time. When does the minibus leave?"

"Ten to eleven," I said.

"Right. I'll be there," promised Jake. He grinned faintly as he added, "Won't old Rusty be surprised?"

As if on cue, Rusty came down the hall on his way to the office. He saw us, though I don't think he heard what Jake had said. Pausing, he raised a questioning eyebrow.

"You two all right?" he asked.

Jake looked him in the eye.

"Fine," he said. "Con had a wee problem and I've been helping her sort it out."

Rusty nodded.

"Good," he said.

As he went into the office, I sensed pleasure in Jake. It mattered that Rusty was trusting him and treating him as a member of the team – though I reckon if Rusty had known the nature of my 'wee problem', he'd have sung a different song. Just then the door of the games room opened and, as people began to wander through the hall, we got up.

"You OK now?" asked Jake.

"Yeah, thanks," I said.

I was about to go off to the dining-room when he called me back.

"Hang on a sec." He drew a small red notebook out of his jeans pocket. "You might give this to Grace when you see her. She dropped it in the dining-room at breakfast time and I found it when I was clearing the tables."

I took the book, which had *Addresses* gold-stamped on the cover.

"Why don't you give it to her yourself?" I asked.

"Fat chance. I might not have Mrs Finch to rescue me next time," retorted Jake.

17

Looking for Harriet

At any time during the past eight years, the idea that I'd ever form a twosome with Piggy Gillanders to fight an evil force would have seemed both incredible and odious. As I got ready for bed, however, I accepted that in two weeks at Weerdwood we'd come a long, long way. I'd been aware of my fear of Jake fading in the face of other terrors, but it was only during our conversation in the alcove that I'd finally admitted that a leopard could change his spots if he tried hard enough. Jake was certainly serious about his education; as a kid he'd communicated by grunts and curses, but now he spoke well and had a wide vocabulary. I'd been really impressed by his knowing about 'co-walkers', and convinced by his sincerity about helping Grace. I wanted to help her too, but I was still very scared. It would be good to have an ally who was older and – let's face it – brighter than me.

That night the clocks were put forward for the start of British Summer Time, so we had an hour less in bed. In the morning most people had trouble getting themselves started, but I'd actually slept longer than usual and got up feeling quite good.

"This is Emily Nichols' birthday," Grace told me when I met her on the stair before breakfast. "Finchy is taking all us QM girls out to lunch at a hotel, then we're going to look at an ancient cathedral. Bet you're green with envy."

It did sound a hell of a birthday treat, yet I was relieved to know that Grace would be away from Weerdwood and under Mrs Finch's eye for the next few hours. She'd been grateful for the return of her address book and seemed quite herself, but you never knew when that might change. By the time I went downstairs at twenty to eleven with Gemma and Gillian, the QM minibus had left and the sun was shining. Willie and a guy called Tim MacGregor joined us and we had a nice little fool-about as we waited for Rusty to take us to church. I had a bad moment when I thought Jake wasn't going to make it, but as Rusty was unlocking the minibus he came loping out, looking quite cool in clean brown trousers and a leather jacket.

"Need a lift somewhere?" asked Rusty innocently.

"Church," said Jake, and they both snorted with laughter.

I hoped this was a sign that there really was less aggro between them.

"Miracles happen," grinned Rusty, switching on the engine. "Everyone belted in?"

As usual, I enjoyed the lively atmosphere of the estuary

as the bus scooted along the waterside. There were golfers on the sandy links, small yachts puffing their sails in the breeze and families out with their dogs along the shore. It was nice seeing ordinary people doing ordinary things. In the plain, quiet interior of the church, I sat between Gemma and Jake. I stood to sing and shut my eyes to pray, but in between I was furtively scanning the walls, looking for a memorial to Lady Harriet Weare. No joy, however. Lady Grace (died 1813), Lady Mary (died 1877) and Lady Charlotte (died 1900) were all commemorated on large plaques crowded with words of praise; they had died young but had time enough to be dutiful daughters, virtuous wives and devoted mothers to their sorrowing children. But the name Harriet was nowhere to be seen.

"Shit," muttered Jake. It wasn't a very nice thing to say in a church, but I understood his frustration. He fidgeted through the sermon, biting his nails and picking his teeth, but at least, I thought with desperate humour, he hadn't peed on the carpet. As we were queuing up in the dusty porch, however, waiting to shake hands with the minister, Jake poked me gently from behind. "Bingo!" he said triumphantly.

Above the door, as if it had been admitted reluctantly and forbidden entry to the church itself, there was a modest grey memorial. It was barely 25 x 20 cm, and this is all it said:

IN MEMORY OF LADY HARRIET WEARE
1896-1914
DEDICATED BY HER BROTHER
21.12.19

"Not much gush there," was Jake's bleak comment.

I'd have liked to talk more with him, but I didn't have a chance. Gillian needed to go to the loo and, by the time we got to the minibus, Willie had settled himself beside Jake. From the seat behind I could hear him droning on about the chances of Heart of Midlothian FC in the Scottish Cup and Jake growling, "Stow it, son. You're boring."

As he climbed out in the courtyard at Weerdwood, Jake said to me over his shoulder, "Speak to you soon." Only he didn't make it happen. I glimpsed him eating his lunch in the kitchen while I was queuing up for mine, but, by the time I'd finished, he was nowhere to be seen.

Sunday afternoon was lightly organised by Weerdwood standards. After lunch, Rusty told us that we could read or play games or watch television – anything, provided we didn't leave the grounds unescorted.

"I'm going for a walk along the shore," he said. "If anyone would like to come, I'll be glad to have you along."

In the absence of the QM girls there weren't many takers. When Rusty set off down the drive only Gillian, Lucy and I accompanied him. There was a definite promise of spring in the air, with a light onshore breeze and a faint warmth in the sun. The hawthorn hedges had a sprinkle of green and the large, sticky brown buds of the horse chestnuts were turning pink at their seams. Once again I felt frustration that the Weerdwood Experience, which had promised so much, had delivered nothing but perplexity and fear. When we jumped down from the path onto the sand the tide was half out. I felt quite envious of Lucy and Gillian as they capered away light-heartedly, picking up shells and chasing each other with strands of wet seaweed. Left alone with Rusty, however, I saw an opportunity. We'd walked a few hundred metres before I plucked up courage to take it.

"Rusty," I said, doing my best to sound casual, "last night when my mum rang, I was in your office. I noticed a picture on the wall above your desk. I wondered if you knew about the woman in it – Lady Harriet. I liked her dog," I added insincerely.

I thought I sounded slightly shrill, but Rusty didn't react. He was looking more relaxed than I'd seen him for a while; his colour was better and his eyelids less puffy. He liked people to take an interest in Weerdwood and he answered with a smile.

"The picture came with the office, actually. I wouldn't have chosen it – I like landscapes better than faces. But the Weerdwood Trust was selling prints of its art collection to raise money at the time, and I think I got that one because nobody else wanted it. The artist isn't rated highly – I've heard he only got the commission because he was engaged to Lady Harriet Weare."

Interesting? I was fascinated.

"Did they marry?" I asked.

Rusty had picked up a pebble and was rubbing it between the palms of his hands.

"I don't think they had time," he said. "The artist, Rupert Molinar, was killed in France during World War I and Lady Harriet died young, like most of the Weares. They weren't a lucky family."

We walked a little further, scrunching along a line of dry seaweed and broken mussel shells. I pondered my next remark but decided that, if there was a risk, it was worth taking.

"I thought she looked like Grace. Lady Harriet, I mean," I said.

I think he genuinely didn't make the connection. He'd said he preferred landscapes to faces, after all.

"Grace," he repeated. "Grace who?"

"Grace Kendrick."

Dropping the pebble, Rusty thumped his forehead with his fist.

"Oh, God!" he groaned. "You mean that poor kid I bawled out for going AWOL. She gave me a hell of a fright, but I must remember to apologise. Is she like Lady Harriet? I can't say I'd noticed, but I suppose she might be. I think Mrs Finch told me there's some relationship."

I didn't think I'd get much further with this one, so I changed tack.

"Do you know what happened to the dog?" I asked.

Just for an instant, I thought this question rattled him.

"I expect its luck ran out," he said shortly, as Lucy and Gillian came running with handfuls of shells for him to identify. "Now then, what have we got here?"

As he began to pick up shells and say, "Cockle, limpet, dog whelk, periwinkle," I could have kicked Gillian and Lucy. If they'd only stayed away another couple of minutes, I could have asked the really intriguing question. What happened to Lady Harriet?

18

The Treasure Hunt

I'd enjoyed Sunday as much as I could enjoy any day at Weerdwood, but I suppose it was hoping for too much that I'd make it through to bedtime without another clash with the abnormal. We'd known since our breakfast briefing that a treasure hunt was planned for the evening and, although I hadn't exactly been looking forward to it, I hadn't been dreading it either.

"It's an event we usually have indoors," Rusty had said, "but there's too much building work going on to make that safe at the moment. Fortunately the weather forecast's good and we have an extra hour of daylight, so we'll be able to hold it in the garden. There'll be a snack in the dining-room at half five and we'll have our proper supper later in the evening."

I can't say I was enthusiastic about being in the garden as night fell, but I comforted myself with the thought that there would be plenty of other people around. Besides, anything was better than looking for 'treasure' in the creepy old house. When we gathered in the dining-room for our snack, I saw Grace sipping Diet Coke and toying with a tiny scrap of quiche.

"I shall never need to eat again," she informed me as I joined her. "I had what looked like a whole chicken and a kilo of vegetables for lunch, and one seventh of a yucky great birthday cake. It's no wonder I'm getting fat."

She was such easy company when she was normal, it was hard to believe there was anything seriously wrong with her.

"What was the cathedral like?" I asked.

"Ruined," replied Grace sweetly. "And how was your day?"

How could I reply? *I've been trying to find out about your ancestor, because she died young and Jake and I think you're in danger of going the same way?* Hardly. I said, "It was OK. I went to church in the morning and after lunch I went for a walk along the beach."

"Oh! Did you see my dog?" asked Grace.

Not so normal, then.

The treasure hunt had been organised during the afternoon by Jess and Miss Gallacher. Just as we were finishing our snack, Jake strolled in.

"Press-ganged to even the numbers," he said, seeing my raised eyebrows. "Bloody waste of time, and me with a biology exam on Friday."

The first thing we had to do was draw folded slips of paper out of a hat to find our partners. I drew Grace and Jake drew Willie, which obviously cheered him up even more.

"No football," I heard him say forbiddingly, "or I may have to put a gag on your face."

Willie laughed good-humouredly.

"The challenge is to complete a crossword," Miss Gallacher explained, as Jess handed out pencils and clipboards, each with a copy of a grid attached. "There are numbered cards pinned up all over the garden. Each one has a puzzle on it, with an answer that fits onto the crossword grid – twelve words across and twelve down. The first pair back in the sitting-room with the crossword completed correctly wins the prize."

I don't think there was ever much chance that Grace and I would win the treasure hunt. She was too grown up not to despise it as a kids' game and my heart just wasn't in it. While other pairs zoomed around the garden, shrieking and eagerly working out codes and jumbled letters and cryptic clues, we got stuck at number three.

"What d'you think 'DOUNF NI LOOSHTED' means?" I asked, as we perched on a carved stone bench. "Six letters, starting with T."

"Who the hell cares?" responded Grace wearily. "Let's just sit here quietly for a while and enjoy the garden."

The keener treasure seekers had drifted away through the gate to the orchard and, as their voices faded and birds made throaty settling-for-the-night noises, I found the garden more melancholy than enjoyable. Damp began to seep through my trousers from the cold bench and I longed to be where it was warm. I fidgeted while Grace sat like a statue, paying me no attention at all.

"I'm freezing. Let's go and see if supper's ready," I said plaintively, but once more Grace had lost the plot.

"This was Rupert's favourite seat, wasn't it, Candace?" she said. "Do you remember how he used to sit here on summer evenings, listening to me playing Schumann's *Träumerei* through the open window?" She heaved a deep sigh as she added, "Poor Rupert! I suppose I must have hurt him very much."

There was frost forming on the grass, but I felt myself beginning to sweat.

"It's cold, Grace. Come inside," I pleaded.

Grace didn't even glance in my direction. As the sky darkened, everyone else was heading back to Admiral's Lodge and I could see the lights from the dining-room casting pale window shapes across the grass. I was both thankful and alarmed when I saw Jake coming alone towards us. I made faces to try to warn him that Grace had gone peculiar and that he shouldn't startle her, but he was clearly intent on something else.

"Have you done twelve down?" he asked abruptly.

"We haven't even done three across," replied Grace, snapping out of her trance as suddenly as she'd snapped in. "Why?"

"Listen to this." Jake took a soiled piece of card out of his pocket. "'Look for the place where grief is not remembered. *Canis fidelis usque ad finem*. Who?'" he read.

It was gobbledygook to me. Grace, however, was now wide awake.

"I know," she said. "I do Latin at QM. It means, 'The dog, faithful right to the end'."

"I know that too," said Jake shortly. "It's the answer to the question 'Who?' that's interesting. Come and look."

Everyone else had gone indoors. There was a babble of voices and the sound of applause from the sitting-room, but the quiet of the garden seemed unaffected as we approached the sundial at the foot of the terrace steps. It came back to me suddenly that I'd once read the motto carved between plinth and pillar, *Time remembered is grief forgotten*, and thought how inappropriate it was to such a sadly haunted place. But unsurprisingly, I had failed to notice the inscription that Jake now pointed out. Grace and I had to squat down and peer closely in the failing light to read the words engraved on a dusty, insignificant plaque near the base of the plinth.

IN MEMORY OF GREY
Canis fidelis usque ad finem
1905-1914

We were straightening up when we became aware of the deerhound, sitting on the edge of a rectangle of light shed by the open glass door. He was watching us with eyes like shining lamps. I gasped in alarm as Grace patted her thigh and said coaxingly, "Come on, Grey! Come on, my good boy!"

The enormous dog pricked up his ears when he heard his name. Scrambling onto his long legs, he uttered a happy yelp and came leaping over the gravel towards us. I was paralysed with terror, but, just as it seemed that the phantom creature was going to hurl himself on Grace, Jake stepped between them. The dog threw himself back on his haunches, his feet skittering on the loose stones at the foot of the steps. For a split second I thought he would turn tail, but this time he didn't. Baring his teeth in rage, he gathered himself to spring at Jake, but Jake was too quick for him. Pushing Grace aside he bounded up the steps and through the open door, banging it behind him in the nick of time.

There was no audible thud as the dog's massive shoulder hit the glass, and only a rush of air as he leapt away and vanished round the corner of the house. But his howls of anger and disappointment were bloodcurdling and seared my head like pain. To my horror, I heard Grace utter a high-pitched giggle.

"Grey never did like Jack," she said callously. "Come to think of it, he didn't like you much either."

19

In Two Minds

By the Tuesday of our last week at Weerdwood, I had only one ambition. I wanted to watch the QM minibus rolling down the drive on Friday morning, carrying Grace Kendrick out of danger and out of my life. After that, other people could be responsible for her – the headmistress at QM, her parents, Mrs Finch, anyone but me. I also had a strong feeling that my ambition wouldn't be realised. Both Grace and I were caught in a ghostly web. It seemed impossible that we'd escape from Weerdwood before something terrible occurred.

During Monday, Grace's condition had deteriorated dramatically. We'd worked together in the garden, trimming the edges of the lawns and raking up the last of winter's withered leaves. Looking round at the neat flowerbeds, weeded paths and clean stonework, it seemed amazing what the wimps' group had achieved in two weeks. Jess was surprised and pleased.

"You've done really, really well," she said. "Thanks to

you, the next group will be able to get straight ahead with the new planting."

The next group. Another crowd of innocents packing their bags and getting geared up for a working holiday in an old country house. The Weerdwood Experience? No thanks.

First thing in the morning, Grace had seemed perfectly OK.

"What are you doing in the Easter holidays, Con?"

"Not a lot. Gillian's having a sleepover for her birthday and her Mum's taking us to *Les Misérables* at the Playhouse. What about you?"

"The Finches have invited me to stay with them in York. Their son Nigel is just a year older than me, so it'll be good fun. Except," added Grace ruefully, "that Finchy is threatening to give me extra maths lessons. She wasn't at all impressed by my last exam results."

"I thought she taught PE," I said, surprised.

Grace giggled.

"You mustn't judge by appearances," she replied.

Of course, it was too good to last. Ten minutes later, as we were carrying a load of leaves to the rubbish heap, I saw the staring expression I dreaded come into Grace's eyes.

"When I first came here from South Africa after Papa died," she said casually, "there were pink roses everywhere. Albertines, I think they were called. Grey used to dig up the bedding plants when he was a puppy. It made the gardener so angry, but he was afraid of Grey. Oh, look, Candace! There's Grey now."

Panic rose in me as I saw the huge dog standing in the

archway that led to the kitchen garden. A repeat of Sunday night's performance wasn't something I relished. But although Grace again called to him, "Come on, Grey! Come on, boy!" the dog seemed more cautious than last time. Although his ears pricked up and his tail lifted, he didn't come to her and, after a moment, he turned and trotted away.

"Hoity-toity!" shrugged Grace. "I expect that silly cook is giving him titbits again."

It went on like this all day, with Grace switching from one personality to another, but spending less and less time as herself. At one moment she'd be talking about Nigel Finch and the cool times she had riding and playing golf with him, the next she'd be calling me Candace, of all ridiculous names, and asking me whether she should wear her white silk dress or her turquoise velvet to the ball at Foulis Castle.

"Rupert's coming from Edinburgh for the ball and bringing my cousin Belle – she's horribly ugly, so she won't be Belle of the Ball. You can come and help me dress, if you like. Jack's driving us in Peter's new Daimler. Rupert won't be pleased, but he'll just have to put up with it."

I wished fervently that someone else would hear her and take fright, but she seemed too crafty for that. If Jess, or even Cameron or Willie came within earshot, Grace would flip from chatter about the deer shoot at Dunrobin, where the Duke had offered to buy Grey for a thousand pounds, to bland remarks about the awful food at QM and her forthcoming trial for the North of England Schools swimming team. At lunch-time I seriously thought of spilling the beans to Mrs Finch, but what was the point? Grace had already seen off Dr Carberry and I had no doubt she would see me off too.

"Con said *what*, Mrs Finch? Poor kid, she needs a holiday . . ."

During the afternoon I heard a great deal about Rupert Molinar and how, after they were married, he was going to build a house at Cap d'Antibes in the south of France, because the light was so wonderful for painting. Jack would go with them as their 'major-domo' and everything would be wonderful, provided there wasn't a stupid war that would ruin everything. The monologue was interspersed with catty remarks that were very un-Grace-like; Belle wouldn't be Belle of the Ball, Candace looked like a mouse with her tail tucked into her bloomers, the cook had fried so much bacon she was turning into a pig.

I was afraid to contradict Grace, partly for fear of another hissy fit, but also in case I might harm her. I'd read somewhere that it's dangerous to wake a sleepwalker abruptly and I thought there might be a parallel here. But as I swept up grass clippings, I wondered bleakly how long it would be before Grace's mind had been taken over completely by Lady Harriet Weare's.

On Tuesday morning, Rusty gave us an outline of the remainder of the week.

"The weather's set fair, so we'll spend the mornings finishing outdoor tasks. This afternoon there'll be an optional visit to the country fair at Poyntz Park, and in the evening we'll have a showing of *The Lord of the Rings*. Tomorrow afternoon we'll go swimming, and in the evening there'll be a special Candlelight Supper with a disco afterwards. That way, on Thursday evening, you can do your packing and have an early night." He grinned round as he added, "You've all worked brilliantly and I hope you're as pleased with your achievements as Jess and I are. You'll get A+ certificates at the end of the week to remind you of your contribution to Weerdwood, and we hope you'll come back sometime and see the results of your hard work."

"God, that guy's a bore," muttered Grace, behind her table napkin. "We had a butler just like him – same name, Cooper, come to think of it."

Jake had been on duty at breakfast-time, but all he'd said to me was, "Sausage or veggie pancake, madam?" As I left the dining-room, however, he poked his head round the door from the kitchen to the hall. "I need to talk to you," he said. "When I was in Inverness yesterday, I found out something interesting. Can you skip the country fair and meet me in the orchard at two o'clock?"

"No problem," I said.

Fortunately for my sanity, that morning Jess had us all together, pricking out seedlings she'd grown in heated propagators in the potting shed. There wasn't much room for six of us at the narrow bench, and the job was so mind-numbingly dull that conversation was limited. The only unpleasant moment was when Willie accidentally upset a seed tray and a lot of the damp compost landed on Grace's lap.

"Whoops! Sorry, Grace," said Willie, who was goofy but nice.

Grace was vile to him.

"You gross idiot," she spat, angrily brushing the compost off her trousers onto mine. "Why do you have to be so bloody clumsy?"

Willie looked gutted.

"I used to like you," he said bitterly.

Grace bit her lip and I could see her fighting back tears.

Sorry, Willie," she whispered, and we all went back to work.

"Are you going to the country fair?" I asked Grace, when we were washing our hands before lunch.

"Yip. And you?"

"Not my kind of thing," I said, although I actually hadn't a clue what a country fair was.

"See you later, then," Grace replied.

To my relief, everyone except Cameron and me had decided to give the fair a whirl. As the minibuses rolled away, he went into the sitting-room to watch telly and I went to the cloakroom and put on my fleece. When I arrived in the orchard Jake was already there, seated on a bench under an ancient grey apple-tree.

"It's nice to get a break from Grace," I said as I joined him. "She's more Lady Harriet than herself now and Lady Harriet's a right pain in the bum. She calls me Candace. I think I'm her servant."

"Join the club," said Jake, with a rueful grin. "Do you want to hear my news?"

"I'm not sure, but I suppose I'd better," I replied.

"Right," Jake said. "Yesterday I had an appointment with my social worker in the morning, then I went to the public library to borrow a book I need for my geography project. While I was there, it occurred to me that I might look up Weerdwood on the internet – I don't have a computer here because I'm still a bad guy and I'm not allowed luxuries. I discovered that the Poyntz District Tourist Board had a website, so I logged on, and there it was. Everything you ever wanted to know about Weerdwood and everything you didn't."

"Like what?" I asked cautiously.

"Like that the present house was built on the site of an old farm called Gabriel's Bank, and Gabriel wasn't a human being at all."

I could feel myself goggling.

"Wasn't a human being?" I repeated.

"No. He was the Angel of Death, and in an old legend 'Gabriel's Hounds' were phantom dogs. When they were heard howling, it meant that someone in the house was about to die, and if you actually saw one – wh-eet!" Jake made a whistling noise and drew his finger across his throat. "Even before Admiral Weare bought it, the place was known to be spooky. His neighbours said he'd bought the curse with the land, and that seems to have been true. In every generation at least two family members died before they were thirty and many before they were twenty. After the death of Lady Harriet Weare in 1914, the family had had enough and they cleared out. That's why the house was practically derelict when the Weerdwood Trust took it over six years ago."

I didn't like what I was thinking. I moistened my dry lips with the tip of my tongue.

"Which means that Grace –"

"Is probably the first person with Weare blood to stay at Weerdwood since World War I," Jake agreed.

"Is Grey one of Gabriel's Hounds?" I asked, shivering.

"It's hard to think otherwise," Jake said.

"Did the website say anything about Gabriel's Flow?"

Jake clicked his tongue impatiently.

"Not a word," he admitted, "and I drew a blank with Lady Harriet too. Nothing about how she died, or why her spirit was confined in a pitch-dark room, or why her dog got a kinder memorial than she did."

It was the memory of the pitch-dark room that overwhelmed me, with its bricked-up window and mouldering but intimate relics of a human life. They could tear it apart and put a lift-shaft through its floor, but nothing altered the fact that it had existed, the saddest room any of us would ever see.

"Oh, Jake," I whispered, "this is terrible. We can't cope alone. Surely there's someone we can tell?"

I would have given anything to push the problem onto an adult, but Jake was adamant.

"There's no one at Weerdwood who would understand," he said. "That may change, but, right now, all we can do is try to watch out for Grace, and for each other. We're in this together and we'll have to see it through."

It wasn't the first time he'd impressed me with brave words. It's only now, with hindsight, that I see how futile they really were. If the curse of Weerdwood had reasserted its power and Gabriel's Hound was on the loose, no amount of kids looking out for each other would make any difference. The past had already begun to repeat itself and it wasn't only Grace who had a role to play.

20

Possessed

The Candlelight Supper, I recollected vaguely from the hype of the Weerdwood information pack, was intended as the high point of our last week. A special feast would be laid on, certificates and prizes would be presented and we could sign up for membership of the Friends of Weerdwood Club. We'd been told to bring something special to wear and I'd packed the dress I'd got for the school Christmas party, a dark blue velvet skirt with a sequinned vest top. Mum said it was too short and Mark said it was too grown up, and I said they should get out more. Since my arrival at Weerdwood it had been hanging at the back of the wardrobe and, when I pulled it out on Wednesday morning, it looked freaky among the jerseys, fleeces and grotty trousers I'd lived in for nearly three weeks. I found my silver sandals too, fragile beside my Timberland boots.

"Have you got a dress for this evening?" I asked Grace, as we came back from our last swim at Poyntz Community Centre.

"Yip, and guess what? It isn't purple," she replied.

Grace had been very quiet all day, but with the abstracted look of someone following routine rather than connecting with what was really happening. I had no idea what was going on in her head, but I suspected that we were in the calm before a storm.

It had been difficult to feel the slightest interest in the Candlelight Supper, with so much else to worry about. The whole Weerdwood Experience had been a disaster for me and I had become deeply irritated by the sight of people enjoying themselves. As I changed into my party dress and listened to the other girls chattering and running to and fro, I felt like screaming and telling them what empty-headed fools they were. What the hell did it matter whether Gillian's black satin trousers looked good with her pink jersey top? Who cared whether Lucy's glitter eyeshadow would be cool with Gemma's grey silk T-shirt? Who did they think they were dressing up for? Rusty? Willie, Kev and Tim of Class 2G? The prospect of smooching with these sweaty, spotty guys in the sitting-room was about as boring as you could get. Yet as I was thinking these things, it occurred to me uneasily that they weren't my kind of thoughts. Normally I loved dressing up and squirting scent and having a giggle with the other girls, and the boys didn't deserve such contempt. Suddenly I saw in my mind's eye a plain girl called Candace, dark-haired and wearing black.

She was sitting on a bed strewn with beautiful dresses, velvet cloaks and furs, watching sourly as beautiful, imperious Lady Harriet Weare got ready to go to a ball.

"Don't you wish you were me, Candace? Don't you wish you were engaged to a handsome young artist, and going to dance all night at Foulis Castle? Oh, go on, admit it. You're sick with jealousy."

If only I'd realised, this mental image was the vital clue to what was going on. I'd had the odd twinge of envy of Grace's model looks and occasionally felt a hard-up teenager's resentment of her Gucci purse stuffed with credit cards. But the sullen, burning jealousy I felt as I thought of Candace was something new. Coupled with my hateful thoughts about my classmates, ought it to have set alarm-bells ringing? I think it almost did. Just for an instant, I wondered if I too had a ghostly co-walker at Weerdwood, someone who wanted to possess my mind as Lady Harriet wanted to possess Grace's. But the idea was too appalling to contemplate and I pushed it away. In that moment, I doomed myself to repeat Candace's mistake.

"May I have a slick of your lip-gloss?" I asked Anne, trying to get into the party spirit.

"Help yourself, Con. Like your dress," she said. "Have you seen the QM girls yet? They're dolled up like in that glossy *Caledonia*. God, these posh people are over the top."

As we went downstairs to the sitting-room, I couldn't help agreeing with Anne. Emily and Isabelle were in front of me, mincing in puffballs of pink and yellow taffeta, like fairies on a Christmas tree. But it wasn't until Grace

Kendrick walked into the sitting-room, alone and last like the Queen, that I knew what 'over the top' really meant.

I never found out where Grace got the dress, but it seems very unlikely that she brought it from school. It's more chilling, but easier to believe that the ghostly Lady Harriet, as well as stealing Grace's mind, had created an illusion of her outward self. The garment was the same in every detail as the one Lady Harriet had worn to be painted by Rupert Molinar, and had still been wearing as her ghost emerged from the haunted room. It was made of paper-white silk, its bodice embroidered with roses and trimmed with streamers of pale pink ribbon. Grace had put up her hair, making herself look older than fifteen, and she was wearing a diamond necklace that looked seriously valuable. There was a moment of dead silence, in which I was aware of Jake's face, white with apprehension, and Mrs Finch's looking puzzled. Then Willie let out a long whistle, the other boys laughed and a scatter of applause acknowledged that we had all been upstaged. Grace smiled complacently.

"Shall we go in to dinner?" she inquired.

Because it was a special occasion, a caterer had been brought in to provide the supper and let Mary and Jake join us. The tables had been pushed together to make one long one, which was covered with a white tablecloth. There were flowers and candelabra like at a wedding reception, place cards with our names and printed menus. Rusty sat at one end of the table and Jess at the other. Mrs Finch, in a black velvet jacket, and Miss Gallacher, in an embroidered caftan, sat opposite each other halfway down. I was seated between

Tim and Cameron, with Jake and Grace across from me. I couldn't avoid watching, with growing consternation, what was going on between them.

At first, Grace seemed put out at finding herself next to Jake who, I must say, was looking cool in a black shirt and grey and white striped tie.

"Why are you sitting down with us?" she asked coldly.

It went through my mind that when Jake was Piggy, her answer would have been a glass of orange juice down her neck, but now he said evenly, "I was invited, ma'am."

"Then I suppose you'll have to stay," conceded Grace with a sly smile.

It usually takes time for a party to get going and, in that respect, this one was typical. By the time we'd finished our cream of vegetable soup, there was a quiet buzz of talk. By the time we'd downed our smoked salmon paté it was punctuated by bursts of laughter and, as the vegetables were being handed round to eat with the chicken kiev, the racket was so loud you could hardly hear what anyone was actually saying. But you didn't have to hear to realise that Grace was getting far closer to Jake than Jake found comfortable. Her face was as flushed as his was pale. In the wavering candlelight, I saw her leaning over to whisper in his ear, then giggling wildly as he removed her hand from his arm and guided it towards her table knife. She didn't pick up the knife and a moment later I knew, from the expression of horror on Jake's face, that her hand was now somewhere other than his arm. To make things even worse, Rusty was watching them with an expression that I interpreted as bad news for Jake.

It was really horrible. Grace was acting completely out of character, but, as Lady Harriet, she wasn't a bit ashamed. Jake sat it out to the end of the meal, but, when Rusty said, "We'll have the prize ceremony after the disco," he couldn't wait to get out of the dining-room. Grace swept after him, and I followed as fast as I could elbow my way round the table. By the time I caught up with them, Grace and Jake were in the alcove outside the office. She was stamping and sobbing with temper and he was holding her by the wrists to stop her slapping his face.

"You have to stop this," said Jake desperately. "You'll get me into terrible trouble. My whole future depends on getting a good report here. If Cooper thinks I've been flirting with you –"

"*Flirting?*" If someone hadn't put on loud music in the sitting-room, the whole house would have heard Grace scream. "You've done more than flirting, Jack Gillanders, and if you think you can walk away from me now, I'll make you sing another song. I'll set my dog on you. I'll tell my fiancé. You'll go to prison –"

At the word 'prison', Jake's face hardened and his pleading manner altered. Slackening his hold on Grace's wrists, he stepped contemptuously away from her.

"Don't threaten me, lady," he said coldly. "I'm leaving Weerdwood, and nothing you can say or do will stop me. And if we're exchanging threats, just remember what I can tell about you – what I shall tell, if you ever come near me again."

For an instant they eyeballed each other silently, then

Grace burst into tears. Flouncing away from Jake, she ran across the hall and up the stair. That was when I again went into Candace's mind and made the mistake she had made long ago. I knew Grace was in trouble and I was supposed to be her friend. I ought to have gone upstairs after her and tried to comfort her. Instead, I felt a mean, nasty surge of pleasure at her despair. She had everything – beauty, fine clothes, money, men making fools of themselves over her – while I was plain and unprivileged, shocked by her behaviour and sick of being patronised. Let her cry, spoilt brat that she was. Why should I care?

When Jake blew out his cheeks and said, "Thank God that's over. Would you like to dance, Miss Carberry?" I grinned and went with him into the sitting-room.

21

Grey

Even after I'd decided I could trust him, I'd never have imagined myself wanting to dance with Jake Gillanders. He wasn't a type I ever fancied – too thin, too colourless, too pinched about the mouth. But the end-of-Weerdwood party spirit was strong and that night a lot of unlikely couples were stomping on the floor – Mrs Finch and Willie, Rusty and Isabelle, Cameron and Jess. Everyone was laughing and I laughed too, but, as the thread connecting me to Candace stretched but didn't break, I wavered between anxiety for Grace and a desire to have a good time. Of course, I assured myself, Grace would have torn off her posh dress in a rage and gone to bed. The best thing was to leave her and give her time to cool down. As soon as this dance session was over, I would nip upstairs and make sure she was OK.

Yet when the music stopped and Jake said, "Jeeze, it's hot in here. Let's go and get some Coke," I followed him towards the dining-room. Even when, out of the corner of my eye, I saw Grey the deerhound prowling restlessly in the hall, I didn't have qualms. Nor apparently did Jake, the one who only yesterday had said we must look out for Grace.

There were a few people already in the dining-room, getting under the feet of the waitresses trying to clear the supper table. The candles were out and the electric lights were on, making everything look messy and tired. Jake brought cans and poured the Coke into tumblers. We were drinking and joshing with Anne and Tim when Mrs Finch came in through the kitchen door. Her kind face was anxious.

"Con dear," she said, "do you know where Grace is?"

The thread between Candace and me snapped suddenly. My stomach tightened and my party spirit died.

"She – she went upstairs," I stuttered. "I think – I don't think she was feeling very well."

"She isn't upstairs now," said Mrs Finch tightly. "I can't find her anywhere."

Jake had put down his tumbler on the table. I'll never forget the horrified look on his face, or my own sudden, sick realisation of what should have been obvious. If Grace and I had ghostly co-walkers, so had he. Jake looked exactly as I felt, as if he had just broken out of someone else's mind – and brought some terrible memory with him.

"Hang on," he said hoarsely to Mrs Finch. "I think I know."

As he crashed through the door into the hall, I ran after him. The dog was gone and I was just in time to see Jake disappearing down the passage to the main house. An instant later the front door banged and a blast of garage shook the sitting-room. I turned and saw Mrs Finch standing behind me. She didn't reproach me, but, as she walked away into the sitting-room, I was overwhelmed with shame. Dazed and frightened, I watched her shaking Rusty's elbow in the hot, disco-lighted room. She practically dragged him into the hall.

"Calm down, Mrs Finch. She can't be far away," said Rusty, but his rapid blinking betrayed his fear.

Before Mrs Finch had time to reply, the passage door banged open and Jake stumbled in. He was panting, his black shirt sweat-stained and clinging to his ribs.

"Gabriel's Flow," he gasped. "She's running down the beach, but I couldn't get to her." He looked straight at Rusty as he said, "*The dog wouldn't let me pass.*"

Mrs Finch looked bewildered, but, as I glanced fearfully at Rusty, I saw pity and understanding in his eyes. That was the moment when the truth dawned on me. Rusty had seen the deerhound too. He touched Jake gently on the shoulder.

"Let's try together, lad," he said.

When they ran, I ran after them, stumbling down the dark drive in my silver sandals, with Mrs Finch pounding at my side. Clear of the trees, a brilliant moon washed out the stars. By its hard green light I could see Grace, a small, white figure standing in the tide swirling over Gabriel's Flow. The water was up to her knees and her arms were waving wildly. A despairing cry rose above the sinister swishing of waves.

"Help! Help! Why doesn't somebody come?"

I could hear Rusty's voice inside my head: *"The tide here is freaky. It flows at a terrifying speed . . . If you were trapped and the tide was coming in, you'd be drowned long before the quicksand closed over you."*

So this was how Lady Harriet Weare had met her death and how Grace must also perish, unless – the solution came to me with sudden, amazing clarity – the spell connecting the two young women could be broken. Which it might be – *if someone succeeded in helping now who had failed to help then*. I don't know if Candace was a brave person. I'm not normally, but at that moment courage kicked in. Stepping out of my sandals, I ran in my tights along the track above the rocks. There were sharp stones, but I felt no pain.

"Grace!" I howled. "Hold on! I'm coming!"

My heroic gesture got no further. As I was about to spring down onto the beach, I felt Mrs Finch's hand grip my shoulder.

"Stop," she said hoarsely. "Let the men try. There's nothing you or I can do."

I didn't argue. Mrs Finch put her arm round me, but her eyes never moved from the forlorn figure on the Flow. Now the water was up to Grace's thighs, eddying around her and snaking further up the beach. She was tearing at her drenched dress, trying to free herself from its clinging folds – a waste of effort, with her feet trapped in the hungry sand. Still, I clung to hope. Even if I wasn't destined to save her, others might be. Rusty and Jake had got the lifebelt from its post and were running through the shallows, uncoiling the rope as they went. By the time they drew level with the warning flags at the edge of the quicksand, they were up to their own knees in the sea.

"Grace!" shouted Rusty. "Catch this and hang onto it!"

The belt went spinning out on the end of the rope, falling just short of the tragic figure. I saw Grace trying to reach it, but the cruel grip of the sand prevented her. Rusty hauled the belt back and this time it was Jake who sent it flying out over the Flow. Again it fell short. I could see it bobbing on the moonlit water, out of reach of Grace's scrabbling hands. The belt was pulled in and thrown a third time, but, just as Grace touched it, it was knocked away by a rolling wave. The sea hissed in triumph and I began to sob silently.

"Grey! Grey! Come to me!"

The despairing voice cried out and, in the moment when human hope died, the dog answered. There was a rush of cold air as he hurtled past us, clearing the rocks in one mighty bound. I felt a vibration as his massive body hit the sand, his feathery paws splaying as he rose onto his long, thin legs. The night was torn by his barking as he galloped into the swirling water. He was immensely tall for a dog, but he was up to his chest by the time he reached the lifebelt and got the rope between his jaws. I held my breath as he moved beyond the red flags. Buoyed up by the water and nudging the belt with his nose, he bobbed and slithered over the volatile sand – until he reached Grace.

The tragic thing was that he should have been able to get back to shore. But as Grace grabbed the rope, ducked and thrust her arms through the belt, Grey did something out of sheer habit. Aware of sand beneath him and expecting approval, he rose on his hind legs and tried to touch her with his paws. He sank suddenly, and I heard a painful yelp of fear. Grace didn't even notice.

"I'm ready," she screamed.

"OK!" shouted Rusty. "Now, Jake – heave!"

As they strained backwards on the rope, Grace came up out of the sand like a mermaid caught in a hoop. But as she slithered through the shallows towards Jake and Rusty, she was more like a seal, her hair and dress plastered to her body and gleaming with silt and sand. The trapped dog threw up his head with a last howl, then a wave crashed over him and he disappeared.

A terrible ending – or so it seemed. As Rusty lifted Grace and carried her out of the sea, Mrs Finch ran to meet them. She walked beside them towards the house, leaving Jake to coil the rope and put the lifebelt back on its hook. That was why only he and I were still on the shore to witness the final reunion between Lady Harriet Weare and her faithful deerhound.

"Grey! Where are you?" The light, clear voice might have been Grace's, but it came from a white, shimmering figure standing on the water's edge, with loops of moon-green foam swirling round her elegantly slippered feet. "Come to me, my good boy!" Grey rose like a star from the waves that lapped over Gabriel's Flow. He was more numinous than I ever remembered him, with drops of water springing like sparks from his silvery coat. Stepping lightly on the sea, he trotted towards his mistress, head and tail held high. She was kneeling in the shallows with her arms stretched out to embrace him; we heard his little, puppy-like moans of pleasure as she took his head lovingly between her hands, fondling his ears and kissing his long, noble nose. "Oh Grey! Never leave me again. I missed you so much!"

Spellbound but unafraid, Jake and I watched as Lady Harriet stood up, brushed down her dress and put her arm round Grey's soft, curly neck. Side by side they walked away along the beach. Beyond Cromar Head, they vanished into history.

22

The Power of Names

When I woke on the morning of my last day at Weerdwood, I was at first amazed to find life continuing as if nothing had happened. As I showered and dried my hair, however, it occurred to me that for the great majority of those in Admiral's Lodge, nothing had. When Jake and I had arrived back from the beach, the party was still in full swing, with disco lights flashing, music thumping, figures waving and jumping up and down. However Rusty had got his dripping burden into the house, they were all too busy to notice. Our haunting remained what it had always been, an intimate, interpersonal affair. Jake and I parted without a word and I went upstairs to take off my dress and bin my broken sandals. I was in my pyjamas when Mrs Finch appeared.

"Con dear," she said rather breathlessly, "are you all right?"

"I think so," I replied. "What about Grace?"

Mrs Finch couldn't hide her sense of averted disaster.

"Amazingly," she said, "I think she's all right too. There are some scratches on her legs and a slight rope burn on one wrist, but she doesn't want to see a doctor. I'll decide about that in the morning, but my hunch is that after a good night's sleep she'll be fine."

"May I see her?" I asked.

"Tomorrow," said Mrs Finch firmly. "You need rest too, so into bed with you." She twitched back my duvet and I crawled in thankfully. "Sweet dreams," she added, in her teachery way, but went on looking down at me. "Con –"

"What?"

"On the shore tonight, did you – um, notice a dog?"

"Yes."

Mrs Finch's large bosom expanded as she let out a great sigh of relief.

"Thank God. I thought I was seeing things," she said.

Rusty didn't appear at breakfast. I was disappointed, because I wanted to see how he looked the morning after the most bizarre party he could ever have organised. Jake, however, was looking remarkably well as he dished up beans and bacon, and so was Grace when she came in with the other QM girls. As I watched her eating cereal, her eyes as bright and her hair as lustrous as if she had hadn't recently been pulled, frightened and mud-slicked, from Gabriel's Flow, I really began to wonder whether the whole evening had been a dream. When Grace caught up with me on the stair and said, " Let's talk later," I thought, *Uh-uh. Back to normal.* Plans to talk at Weerdwood had a way of being thwarted. What I could never have guessed was who would thwart them now.

It was the last day of March and spring in the garden had really arrived. Pink and white flowering currants were in bloom, early daffodils were bursting and little blue hyacinths were poking through the crevices in the walls. Bare branches wore a suggestion of leaf and the long chimneys of Weerdwood rose serenely into a pale blue sky. There was no dog to watch me and no brooding, ghostly presence. This was the Weerdwood I'd yearned for, and I had a moment of sadness because I'd never know it this way.

"I'm going to prune some roses," said Jess, drawing on her leather gloves. "Cameron and Willie, you'd better help me, since you're going to miss me so much tomorrow. Girls, I'll give you some summer bulbs to plant. Fifteen centimetres deep, ten apart, OK?"

She was so calm, so prosaic, I wondered whether she had any idea that her fiancé had been seeing a phantom dog, or that last night he'd had to rescue one of his charges from a death that would have blown their life at Weerdwood apart. Questions, questions and, with so little time in hand, probably not much chance of ever knowing the answers. At least, that's what I was thinking when, about ten o'clock, Jess sent me with a message to Miss Gallacher, who was working on the other side of the house. I was on my way back when a blue car drew up behind the minibuses and a woman in a fawn suede coat got out of the driver's seat. She was thin and dark, with greying hair knotted at the crown of her head and a brown, prematurely lined face. But her eyes were a nice shade of green and she had a pleasant smile.

"Can you help me?" she asked. "My name is Judith Kendrick. I've come to see my daughter."

"Eh?" I knew I was goggling like Homer Simpson, but I couldn't help it. My voice came out in a breathless squeak. "She's in the garden. I'll take you –"

Only, of course, the former Judith Weare knew where the garden was. She began to run and I caught up just in time to see what I wouldn't have missed for anything, the sight of Grace hurtling across the lawn into her mother's arms.

I hadn't expected to spend my last Weerdwood evening in a chic hotel restaurant in Poyntz with Jake Gillanders, Grace Kendrick and her mother. But then, when had anything happened at Weerdwood that I expected? The restaurant was a cool place, with crisp blue tablecloths, arty seascapes and fishing nets draped across the ceiling.

"Have what you like, but I'm going to have fish and chips," said Mrs Kendrick. "It's the kind of thing you miss in India."

She was easy without being matey, and didn't embarrass Jake and me by inviting us to call her Judith. According to Grace, Rusty had also been invited, but said he had to spend the last evening with the other kids. I reckoned that, since Mrs Kendrick had spent an hour closeted with Rusty and Jess in the afternoon, they might already have said all they had to say. Grace and I had used the hour to do our own packing, though she kept wandering through to my room with a dazed, happy expression on her face.

"Can you believe it?" she said. "Mum came all the way from India because she knew I was in trouble and she wanted to be with me. The minute she got the e-mail Jake sent her from the library, she just got on a plane and came. What a good thing I dropped my address book in the dining-room, otherwise Jake would never have known where Mum was."

So that was one minor mystery solved. But I had a big question burning a hole in my mind and, when Grace was sitting on the side of my bed, I grabbed the opportunity to ask it.

"What do you remember about last night?"

Grace considered for a moment, then she said, "I remember being Harriet Weare. Ever since I saw her ghost coming out of the walled-up room, I've had moments of thinking I was her, but I was scared to tell anyone in case they thought I'd gone mad. The last few days it's been getting worse, and by last night I couldn't remember ever being me. I *was* Harriet Weare, and I thought you were the doctor's daughter and Jake was Jack, my brother's footman, with whom –" she flushed in embarrassment "– I was insanely in love. I'd got dressed to go to a ball with my fiancé Rupert Molinar, but there was a dinner party here at Weerdwood first. In the dining-room I was flirting wickedly with Jack to annoy Rupert, but he wasn't half as annoyed as Jack. After dinner he followed me into the hall and we had a flaming row, with me trying to pull rank and him snarling that he was leaving Weerdwood and I couldn't stop him. That was when I realised he didn't love me at all, and all my batty plans for our future were in vain. I was so distraught that I ran out of the house and down onto the

155

shore – I was shouting for Grey but he didn't come and that made me worse. I could hardly see for crying and I suppose that's why I blundered onto the quicksand – it had no warning flags long ago. By the time I felt the sand sucking at my feet, it was too late. I knew the tide was coming in."

"Do you remember," I asked carefully, "whether anyone tried to rescue you?"

Grace nodded thoughtfully.

"I remember," she said, "Rupert and Candace standing on the rocks and Jack Gillanders and the butler Cooper running down the shore. I heard them shouting and I think they tried to throw a rope, but I couldn't reach it. It was when I screamed for Grey that I suddenly became me again, and saw that Jake and Rusty had a lifebelt. But it was Grey who saved me, wasn't it, Con?"

"Yes," I agreed. "Poor dog, he must have died trying to rescue Harriet. Perhaps he was ashamed of his failure and when he saw you in the Flow he thought he was getting a second chance. When he succeeded, the spell of the past broke. Grey is happy and you're free, because Harriet isn't interested in you any more."

It was the best I could do, and Grace didn't probe further.

"When Mum took me out for lunch earlier," she said, "I decided to tell her everything. Better coming from me than from someone else. She was in an awful tizz when I described what happened last night, but when she'd calmed down she didn't seem totally surprised. She said she was in a blind panic when she wrote to me and afterwards she felt awful. She'd have come sooner, only my dad kept telling her not to be silly, because the Weerdwood ghosts were just stupid superstition. This evening, she's going to tell us all she knows."

We all had fish and chips and ice cream, then we moved into the bar where there was a log fire and comfortable seating. Mrs Kendrick ordered coffee for herself and hot chocolate for us, and we sat together very comfortably. But it was twenty to eight; time was getting short and there was a lot I wanted to know.

"Mrs Kendrick," I said, to set the ball rolling, "do you know about Gabriel's Hounds?"

To my surprise, she laughed.

"Wild geese," she said. "That's what 'Gabriel's Hounds' were originally. Long ago, when people heard them honking overhead in the dark, they were frightened, and the superstition arose that they were phantom hounds hunting for lost souls to take to their master, the Angel of Death. At Weerdwood, of course, events seemed to prove the legend and it took a strong grip on local people's imagination. There was even a rhyme about it:

> *When Gabriel cries*
> *Over bank and on brae,*
> *The children of Weerdwood*
> *Shall all wede away.*"

"Does 'wede' mean 'die'?" I asked.

"Yes. And they did," Mrs Kendrick told me.

"Yet you don't believe that the Weares were cursed?" inquired Jake curiously.

"Oh, but I do," said Mrs Kendrick emphatically. "They were cursed all right, but not by phantom hounds howling in the night. The curse of the Weares was hereditary heart disease, which killed three in five of them before they were thirty. My father didn't have it, nor do I, which is why I thought it was safe to have Grace. Mercifully, because of modern surgery, she's been completely cured, but earlier generations weren't so lucky."

Which was a convincing debunking of the supernatural, as far as it went, and it was good to know that Grey wasn't one of Gabriel's Hounds after all. But as Grace lightly touched her mother's hand and I saw the scar of the rope on her wrist, last night's terrifying events flicked like a horror movie through my head. Even if Gabriel's Hounds and the curse of the Weares could be explained naturally, there were still big questions to be answered. Jake, however, wasn't yet ready to move on.

"This heart problem," he said. "Did Lady Harriet Weare have it?"

"Indeed she did," replied Mrs Kendrick. "She and her twin brother Peter were orphaned by the death of their father in the Boer War in 1902. They were sent to Weerdwood to live with their much older brother Angus, who had inherited the title. Harriet was a very difficult, bad-tempered child, but Angus knew she'd little chance of reaching maturity and he spoilt her dreadfully. She grew up arrogant, conceited and self-centred – hateful to her brother Peter and cruel to her cousin Belle – Isabelle Clifford, who was my grandmother."

Grace, no doubt remembering the fight in the passage, rolled her eyes and put her finger to her lips. I couldn't help grinning, but Mrs Kendrick was too intent on her story to notice.

"Harriet had a destructive personality. She saw people as rivals and the only good relationship she ever had was with her dog. When she was sixteen, Angus commissioned the artist Rupert Molinar to paint her portrait. She was very beautiful and the poor man fell head over heels in love with her. They became engaged, but that didn't stop Harriet having a passionate love affair with the footman, Jack Gillanders. I don't suppose he was blameless, but I've always felt sorry for him. With an unstable young woman like Harriet, he was damned if he did and damned if he didn't. Anyway, it seems that by the spring of 1914 Rupert Molinar had got wind of what was happening – Angus reckoned he'd been tipped off by Harriet's so-called friend, the doctor's daughter Candace Carberry. There were awful rows, and Rupert was about to call off the engagement when Harriet saved him the trouble by getting herself and her dog drowned in Gabriel's Flow."

"I once dreamed I saw you at the window of Harriet's room," I remarked to Jake. "Only now I see it wasn't you at all."

Before he could reply Grace, who had been contentedly sharing a sofa with her mother, intervened for the first time.

"Mum," she said, "if Harriet Weare didn't actually die in her bedroom, why was it walled up?"

An expression of horror crossed Mrs Kendrick's thin face. As she poured herself another cup of coffee, I noticed a tremor in her hand. But she steadied herself and continued calmly.

"Until Harriet died, Weerdwood was a sad house. Afterwards, it became a seriously spooky one. Angus hadn't married and, after Harriet's brother Peter joined the navy and the younger menservants went to war in 1914, he was left alone with the butler, a man called Robert Cooper." Jake's eyebrows shot up, but Mrs Kendrick didn't pause. "Almost immediately, both men began to hear noises in Harriet's room above the front door. She had a piano in there and they'd hear it being played, and the sound of laughter and her voice singing. And there was the dog, Grey. Angus and the butler saw the dog everywhere, in the garden, in the house, on the shore. They couldn't sleep for its howling in the night and yelping outside the door of Harriet's room. Nor were they the only ones to suffer. Candace Carberry was so tormented by Harriet's ghost that she had a nervous breakdown, and Jack Gillanders told Cooper in a letter from France that he was more afraid of a phantom deerhound than he was of the Germans.

"During and just after the war, a string of tragedies occurred. Peter Weare, Rupert Molinar and Jack Gillanders were all killed in battle. Candace Carberry was sent to a mental hospital by her father and Robert Cooper hanged himself in the wood. Poor Angus couldn't take any more. He erected memorials to Harriet and her dog and had the haunted room sealed up – it now seems with Harriet's ghost inside."

"Hang on a minute," interrupted Jake. "That's something

I've never understood. How could a ghost be walled up? I thought the whole point was that they could walk through things."

Mrs Kendrick frowned.

"Yes, I see what you mean," she said.

There was a moment of perplexed silence. It was Grace who broke it.

"I think – perhaps she wasn't walled up at all," she said. "We know that, although they died together, her spirit couldn't find Grey's, which perhaps was the price she had to pay for being so proud and unkind when she was alive. I think that when the voices she knew had fallen silent and she realised she was left all alone, she chose to hide herself away in the room where she'd been happy and which still had her familiar things inside it. I reckon she hid there for years and years and years, until at last the door was forced open and she had to leave. Poor thing – she must have been so lonely and afraid."

I'd never thought I could pity Lady Harriet Weare, but now I wanted to cry. I changed the subject quickly.

"What happened to Angus, Mrs Kendrick?" I asked.

I sensed she was glad to change the subject too.

"He went to live in London," she told me. "After Peter's death he had no direct heir, so he used his money to found the Weerdwood Trust. The Weares have never lived at Weerdwood since, although the house remained family property until quite recently. When I was a child I used to spend occasional holidays with my parents in a cottage on the estate, and I remember so clearly the terror of that bricked-up window and the awful desolation of the place. When I learned that Grace was here I was appalled, though not half as appalled as I am now."

She bit her lip and blinked tears out of her eyes. I waited until she'd drunk some more coffee then I said, "There's just one more thing I'd like to know. I can see that what happened to Grace was because she's related to Lady Harriet and looks like her. But why Jake and Rusty and me? Do you think we're related to people in the past too?"

Mrs Kendrick looked at me pensively.

"I suppose it's possible," she said. "But it's also possible that the past has a memory capable of being roused simply by the power of names. You can find out if you want to, but my advice is to let it go. Families like mine are fixated on the past and it isn't healthy. What young people need is a future."

I thought these were wise words. Jake, however, had something else on his mind.

"Mrs Kendrick," he said, "will Rusty lose his job?"

His anxious look told me I'd been right in thinking his relationship with Rusty had improved. I was glad, because, though sometimes boring, Rusty was a good guy really. Mrs Kendrick obviously agreed.

"Of course not. He's a splendid young man," she said warmly. "It wasn't his fault that he had to take over a haunted house, and he's no more to blame for being called Cooper than you are for being called Gillanders. Rusty admits he made mistakes – or rather that smarty-pants he's engaged to says he did – like inviting you all to the opening of the haunted room and trying to head off trouble by forbidding you to mention dogs. Maybe he was less than truthful, but he genuinely thought no one else could see the deerhound. Jess didn't, nor did Mary or any of the people who brought groups to the house. The young woman who drowned some years ago had a history of running away, and the shopkeeper at Poyntz Store admitted he'd been winding the Cub Scouts up about ghosts at Weerdwood. The only way Rusty could be in trouble would be if I complained about what happened last night, which I certainly won't do. He did all he humanly could to look after you all, and I owe him – and you, Jake – a debt I can never repay."

"He'll be OK now," said Jake. "We all will, because last night Harriet and her dog found each other and left Weerdwood for good. Con and I saw them go."

23

Temporary Friends

It would be nice to say that the bond formed at Weerdwood between Jake, Grace and me was permanent, that we talked and sent each other text messages and met up from time to time. Only it didn't work out that way and, to be honest, it was never on the cards that it would. On the morning when we brought down our rucksacks and heaved them onto the minibus, there was a lot of running about in the courtyard, exchanging addresses and mobile numbers, hugging and promising to keep in touch. Jake had come out of the house with Rusty, Jess and Mary to see us off. He and I said goodbye amicably, but I think we both acknowledged that forgiving is easier than forgetting. Outside the enclosed, intimate world of Weerdwood, our traumatic childhood would always cast a shadow between us.

He said, "Say 'Hi' to your Mum from me," and I said,

"Good luck in your exams." We slapped palms casually and I waved to him from the window of the minibus.

I did hear from him once after that. He sent me a postcard saying that he'd got the Higher grades he needed and was going to Liverpool University to read geography. I remembered that Liverpool was where his girlfriend had a place and I was pleased for him. He really had turned his life round and he deserved a break.

I'd have been sadder if I'd thought, as the minibus hit the road south, that Grace too had been only a temporary friend. We hadn't had much time to say goodbye, because a taxi had arrived to take Jake and me back to Weerdwood; Grace and her mother were spending the night at the hotel and driving south together the next day. As I put on my jacket in the cloakroom, Grace was bubbling with excitement and happiness.

"Mum and Dad have decided to leave the work in India to younger people and run their charity from London," she told me. "They want to have me with them and get to know me properly before I'm grown up." A bit late in the day, I thought, but it was no business of mine. "I'm to stay at QM until the end of next term, then I'm going to live at home and take my A-levels at St Paul's." (I hadn't a clue what St Paul's was, but I found out later that it was the poshest girls' day school in London. Now there was a surprise!) "Mum and I are going to look at houses in the holidays," Grace said, as we walked to the front door where Jake was waiting. "I have your address and as soon as I know mine, I'll write."

Only she never did. Mum, to whom I had given a

severely censored account of the Weerdwood Experience, got quite steamed up when no letter came. She muttered about posh people thinking they were celebrities and being too grand for the likes of us, but I never thought that about Grace. OK, my dreams of her coming to stay in our cramped little bungalow and me taking her to Edinburgh Castle and the Royal Yacht *Britannia* were a bit unrealistic, as were my dreams of swanning round Harrods and Harvey Nichols with her. But Grace wasn't a snob, and I don't believe she had the kind of second thoughts Mum was suggesting.

I suspect that, despite having been so calm immediately after her ordeal, Grace probably had a whopping delayed reaction to her haunting at Weerdwood. God knows, what happened to me was frightening enough. I'll never forget the ghastly realisation, on the night of the Candlelight Supper, that I too had a co-walker who wanted to influence my mind. It only lasted a few hours for me, but Grace had been tormented for days and knew that – however briefly – she had actually become another person. I reckon she didn't get in touch because she couldn't bear to meet up with someone who would remind her of her appalling experience, and how she'd come within a hair's breadth of sharing the fate of Lady Harriet Weare. I'm glad she had her parents to support her, but, now that I've written everything down, I don't think I'd want to see her again either.

I still have one contact with Queen Maud's College, though. Every year, Mrs Finch sends me a Christmas card.

"Con, I hope you are fine and getting on well at school. Best wishes, K Finch."

To which I reply, "I'm very well and school is fine. Best to you and Mr Finch. Love from Con."

It isn't much, but it's nice. She and I did see a ghost together, after all.

Miss Gallacher still takes groups from Underwood Academy to Weerdwood, only now they go to partner disabled kids, not to paint and work in the garden. They go sailing in the estuary, camp out in the woods and have barbecues at Sutor Point – the sort of activities I'd enjoy anywhere else. Rusty and Jess are married and, Miss Gallacher says cryptically, happy in their own way.

I like to think that on summer evenings Weerdwood is the way I dreamt it, with music and laughter floating from open windows across the lawn. I can shut my eyes and visualise the old house cleaned and restored, its ghosts exorcised and its terrible past forgotten. I imagine the garden as I never saw it, full of lupins, hollyhocks and poppies, their colours intensifying as night draws in from the sea. I'm sorry that I never saw the seals and dolphins beyond Sutor Point and I hope that, wherever they are, the ghosts of Lady Harriet and Grey are happy together.

One day last week, Miss Gallacher stopped me in the school corridor.

"Con," she said, "I'm taking names for the Weerdwood trip next term. Gillian's going to front up the team. Why don't you come along as her assistant?" *The story of my life.* "It's your last year at school and your last chance," added Miss Gallacher coaxingly. "Rusty and Jess would be so pleased to see you, and you wouldn't recognise the place. The staircase has just been restored, and Rusty found replica peacock wallpaper for the drawing-room. I think even the Weares would be impressed."

Was I tempted? *Not.*

"Sorry. I've put my name down for the French exchange," I said.

THE END